My (Almost)
Hikikom

ALEXANDRO CHEN

ALEXANDRO CHEN

ISBN 9781720097822

Edited by Diamaya Dawn

CONTENTS

KFC B&B

Kazumi had stayed in this KFC for five days straight. Her stomach was stuffed with fried chicken, her scalp sleek with cooking oil, her white "Nugs Not Drugs" T-shirt smeared with unwashable ketchup stains. This pitiful state made her hungry for her apartment in Shinjuku.

No, she couldn't go back.

Better eat these thoughts away. From her Mighty Bucket, she picked a drumstick and nibbled on it. Despite being the tenth she'd eaten today, she enjoyed the explosion of crispness and juiciness.

Perhaps the primary fuel of the human body was slowly shifting to fast food.

Kazumi needed not only food but also shelter and proper hygiene. Luckily, she'd found this twenty-four-hour KFC, where she could sleep safely on the tables and wipe her body with moist tissues in the bathroom. In the wee hours, she would stick her head in the sink and wash her hair with liquid soap.

A viable routine—if not for the clerk with the name tag Ikeda.

He stood at the counter, craning his stick-thin neck in her direction and squinting his owl-like eyes. As always.

This time, Ikeda circled the counter and ambled toward her. At her table, he adjusted his navy blue KFC cap. "Sorry for bothering you, but have I seen you before?"

Kazumi glued her back to the chair, facing the full-wall window. "Maybe. I'm a regular customer." Even without looking, she sensed his large eyes on her. Scanning. Scowling. Doubting. When would this jerk clerk go away?

Ikeda must have read her thoughts. "Sorry for interrupting," he said and dashed back to his post.

She heaved out a sigh. *So good.*

Have I seen you before? These words stirred tormenting memories in Kazumi, like film scenes her mind forced her to watch. Unfortunately, closing her eyes would be useless.

The first frames showed her sitting at the oval table of a McDonald's, waiting for her date and university classmate, Daiki. Although swallowing hamburgers and sipping Cokes wasn't her idea of a romantic evening, she looked forward to spending time with him. Daiki was good-looking, easygoing, quick-witted, and down-to-earth.

Everything except punctual.

Kazumi glanced at her phone for the eighth time. The screen's digits displayed ten past seven, twenty minutes after the agreed time. Better text him.

Afraid of meeting me? Don't be a chicken!

She winced at her distasteful joke—a facial expression that deepened when another twenty minutes passed, and Daiki still hadn't called her. Where could he be? Thousands of thoughts surfaced in Kazumi's neural ocean. Thoughts that found an outlet as text messages.

Did you get lost?

Did you get in a car accident?

Did you get tired of me?

At eight, driven by a twinge of hunger, Kazumi staggered to the counter and came back to her seat with a McDouble to start her one-person date.

Chewing on her cheeseburger, she weighed the implications of Daiki's absence. Perhaps he hadn't meant it when he said, "We can meet at McDonald's tomorrow." Even though Kazumi had meant it when she said, "Sure, I've been craving junk food!" Okay, she hadn't. She'd just been happy about his invitation. In the future, she should view happiness as a Happy Meal. Fleeting. Unhealthy. For children.

"Excuse me," said a voice. "Have I seen you before?"

Kazumi looked up from her McDouble. A man. His flat forehead, thick neck, and hefty body made her think of a bull—which didn't mean he looked like a beast. On the contrary, those features gave him some sort of wild masculine beauty.

"Maybe," she replied. "I'm a regular here."

"I don't come here often. Maybe I saw you somewhere else?"

Kazumi got that a lot since she had an average face. An average nose, an average mouth. Her only atypical characteristic—that set her apart from other Japanese girls—was her weight. However, she didn't classify herself as "fat" but "curvy."

"I remember now!" the guy blurted. "You're Kazumi."

She blinked at him. "And you are ...?"

He touched his chest. Even his hand was muscular. "Hidehiko."

"I still don't—"

8

"I attend Keio University too," he explained. "You probably don't know me. I keep a low profile—and attendance rate."

Kazumi stared, puzzled.

Hidehiko scratched his coiled hair. "Sorry, I'm not explaining myself well. I don't really know you, but I know someone who does. Daiki."

"You know Daiki!" Kazumi rose from her chair.

"Yeah ..." He took a few steps back, probably shaken by Kazumi's explosive response. "In fact, I just ate brunch with him."

"What? It can't be ..."

"I know, who the hell eats brunch for dinner? We couldn't find anything else."

She shook her head. "I mean, he was supposed to meet me."

"Oh," Hidehiko said, as though he'd been responsible for the misdeed. "So, Daiki wasn't lying after all—at least not to me."

"Lying?"

"Can I order first?" He rubbed the chiseled abs beneath his shirt. "The brunch didn't fill me up. And the story might take some time. But don't worry, I'll try to make it fast."

After Hidehiko ordered a Teriyaki Burger at the counter, they sat across each other at the oblong table. Two strangers sharing a familiar meal.

"I shouldn't talk about this, but Daiki shouldn't have stood you up." Hidehiko fiddled with his burger box, as though not daring to open it. "Truth is, he had planned to meet you, but changed his mind after a friend commented that you looked a little—*plump*."

Kazumi grimaced. "Daiki's friend wasn't talking about my lips, right?"

"I'm afraid not ..."

She pushed aside the tray with her half-munched cheeseburger and buried her face in her crossed arms. How about going on a diet? Or even better, starve to death?

"Please don't put too much weight on Daiki's thoughts," Hidehiko said, his voice reaching her stung ears. "He bases his life on what other people say."

"But everyone does that. Besides, I *am* a bit fat."

"You're not. Models in magazines and on TV are too thin, together with the women who worship them."

"Then what am I?" Kazumi raised her head, her eyes blurry.

Hidehiko beamed at her. "You're the *right* size. Don't let anyone tell you that you're wrong."

She gaped at the guy, not really looking at him but at the reality he had destroyed. No, reconstructed. People had given her many bricks before, but she needed this last one to finish the whole structure.

Kazumi dragged her tray in front of her and took a bite of her McDouble, glad she wouldn't have to eat the rest alone.

After that first encounter, Kazumi and Hidehiko started meeting regularly at the McDonald's. Once they got tired of fast food, they switched to more traditional alternatives like salmon sashimi, soba noodles, and curry rice. When meeting to eat didn't satisfy them anymore, they moved their encounters to shopping malls, parks, and—when the right time came—to Hidehiko's apartment.

Eventually, not even sleeping together fulfilled them. They craved to wake up in each other's arms, to have their favorite face greet them every morning.

And so, when Kazumi and Hidehiko reached the second year of their relationship, they moved into a one-bedroom apartment, paying the rent with their part-time jobs in fast food restaurants. Kazumi couldn't have been happier (she had even begun to enjoy Happy Meals). Happiness, however, came with a price: the fear of losing it.

"Sure you're not gonna get fed up with me?" Kazumi turned sideways to face Hidehiko on the futon.

He wrapped his naked body around hers and kissed her. "Never. I'd come to eat you again and again, even if you become bad for my health."

"Not true. Everyone gets sick of unhealthy food."

"Are you sick of it?"

Kazumi chewed this over. "Kinda."

"Then how about we eat healthy?" Hidehiko suggested.

"All right." Kazumi welcomed the idea. Cooking together was one of the most intimate activities you could do with a partner. But what to prepare?

The healthiest food, they read on the Internet, were homemade meals. Kazumi and Hidehiko followed this advice. They spent their evenings cooking pasta carbonara, paella soup, nigiri sushi—everything from an article called *100 Dishes to Cook Before You Die*.

Eating healthy made Kazumi lose so much weight, she acquired the physique of a TV or magazine model. It delighted and motivated her to finish the whole list.

Unfortunately, she never did.

"Excuse me," said a voice, dragging Kazumi out of her sour reminiscing.

When she gazed up, she was greeted by the picture of Colonel Sanders. Could it be his ghost talking? Strange, he sounded familiar.

"Sorry to bother you." Ikeda put down the chicken bucket he'd been holding on the table. Probably someone's order. "But I *really* think I've seen you before."

The scare shook Kazumi's numbness away. "M-maybe. I came here yesterday."

"And the day before, and the day before that."

Kazumi sighed. The clerks in this KFC would eventually become suspicious of her.

"Look." Ikeda sat across from Kazumi, a reproachable action if a manager saw. He seemed unconcerned. "I'm not going to ask you to leave. This is a twenty-four-hour KFC after all. You're free to stay as long as you want." He narrowed his huge eyes. "I just wonder if you have *another* place to stay. You don't look like a homeless person."

Kazumi faced the full-wall window.

"Look," Ikeda began, "if you're being *mistreated*—"

"It's not that."

Nodding, Ikeda placed his hands flat on the square table. "In that case, you know, no matter what problems you have at home, you can go back. Because that's the definition of home—the place where you can always return to."

"I don't have a home," Kazumi said. "Just an apartment."

"An apartment works too, no?"

"You don't understand ..."

"Maybe someone else will? A friend?" In a low, almost inaudible voice, he added, "Or your boyfriend?"

She softened to him. For the first time, Ikeda didn't seem to be looking *at* her, but *after* her. "No, my boyfriend wouldn't understand."

"But he must be worried ..."

"He doesn't know I left the apartment." Kazumi scowled at her empty chicken bucket. "Because he left the apartment too. Forever."

"I understand now." Still sitting, Ikeda bowed low. "Sorry, I didn't mean to pry into your private life."

"It's okay. I'm in a public place."

"In that case, I advise you to go back to your apartment. I understand it's not a home anymore, but you can turn it into one again. You can't do that at KFC. True, it's open twenty-four hours, but it isn't a good idea to stay here twenty-four seven."

Kazumi clutched the edge of her chair, shuddering. "I don't want to spend even a minute in that apartment."

"May I ask why?"

She shifted her hands from the chair to her eyes, blocking out every particle of light. "Because everything in the apartment reminds me of my ex-boyfriend! The futon, the kitchen, even the chopsticks. And his smell is all over the place. It won't go away. No matter how much I wash it." Kazumi leaned on the table, the weight of anxiety lifting off her shoulders.

"I'm sorry." Ikeda offered a bow, almost touching the table. "I *really* shouldn't have pried into your private life."

"It's okay," Kazumi said. "I was waiting for a chance to share this with someone. After all, this is the longest I've spent being alone—alone among people."

"Don't tell me you haven't spoken to anyone ..."

Kazumi nodded. "Since *that* day."

Exactly a week ago, Kazumi and Hidehiko had been discussing his gradual withdrawal. More and more, he made excuses for not cooking at home and eventually for not eating out with her. Instead, he would go to restaurants, bars, and izakaya with his friends. Or a secret second girlfriend.

"You finally got fed up with me, right?" Kazumi asked Hidehiko one night.

"It's not that," he replied without rolling around. His back had become a familiar sight, one that made her boyfriend seem like a stranger. "It's just that we are soon graduating and starting a new life. Aren't you hungry for new things?"

"I am. But I want to share those meals with you."

"Hey, wanna eat hamburgers for breakfast? At MOS Burger?"

Kazumi went there with him, smiling. Hidehiko probably wished to rekindle the fire they once had. The fire that had cooked their food and given them candle-lit dinners.

Wrong. It was their last supper. And that day, he didn't return to their apartment.

"I lied to you," Hidehiko said in their post-goodbye phone call. "I came back home, not because my mom couldn't get out of bed, but because I had to get out of the apartment. The thing is, I can't live with you anymore. I'm sorry." He hung up. And while Kazumi stared at her phone in a stunned stupor, he sent a text.

You can keep all my stuff: my laptop, my books, my clothes. Please, accept them as an apology gift. And sorry again.

Kazumi didn't reply to her boyfriend—or rather ex-boyfriend's—message. Instead, she stayed at MOS Burger, analyzing Hidehiko's abandonment over and over. No, starting a new life couldn't have been the whole reason. Hidehiko should've been cooking a bigger plan. Or a more rotten one.

A few hours later, Fukumi, a friend of her ex-boyfriend and lover of fast food, spotted Kazumi and sat with her to talk about Hidehiko. She knew about their recent separation.

"I don't usually reveal my friend's secrets." Fukumi munched her French toast. After swallowing, she continued, "But this isn't a secret. It's a crime. And I'm not sure if I wanna be Hidehiko's friend anymore."

Kazumi blinked at her. "Why? What happened?"

Fukumi explained that Hidehiko was dating a girl from their university. That they'd been going to restaurants, bars, and even to Hidehiko's home.

"And that's not the most horrible part," Fukumi said, putting down her fast-food breakfast. "I heard that Hidehiko left you because someone told him you'd become *bony*. Like TV and magazine models."

Gawking at her, Kazumi tried to swallow down the truth. It hurt. More than trying the same with a fish bone. "And the other girl is—?"

Fukumi nodded. "She's the shape Hidehiko likes. Similar to yours when you guys began dating."

Back at her apartment, Kazumi didn't phone Hidehiko to pour a rain of reproach on him. Instead, she went out and wandered gloomily the kaleidoscopic streets of Shinjuku.

At some point, she spotted a KFC, one that operated twenty-four hours. And an idea cooked in her mind. One so delicious, it might wash away the bad taste in her mouth. And it did.

Until today.

Without a word to Ikeda, Kazumi grabbed the tray with the leftovers of her Smoky Grilled chicken and dumped it into the bin. Then she shouldered her satchel.

"You leaving?" Ikeda asked, his eyes wider than ever.

With a nod, she ambled to the glass door, looked over her shoulder, and said, "I'm tired of chicken."

I DON'T WANT TO KILL MYSELF, REALLY

Everyone thinks I want to kill myself. Not their fault. I've gotten into a few too many accidents this year.

Like the time I fell from the balcony of my four-story apartment. Luckily, I survived with only a broken ankle and a horrified landlady.

And a skeptical girlfriend.

"Sure it was an accident?" Ai bawled, clutching my hospital gown.

I sat up on the bed, careful not to shift my plaster cast, and placed my hand on her shoulder. "Look, I was hanging my clothes on the laundry pole. There was a gust of wind and my favorite T-shirt—the one that says, 'Love Life'—flew off. I tried to catch it but fell from the balcony.

"You know the rest. I was saved by a mattress someone wanted to throw away, the owner called the ambulance—he also thought I jumped intentionally—and now I'm here. Safe. I was lucky."

Ai gazed up at me. Her sad, round eyes always reminded me of a puppy—defenseless and requiring delicate handling.

This time I had managed her well; her tears dried and her mouth curved into an incandescent smile. The smile that helped me to wake up in the morning and fall asleep at night. That reminded me that darkness was just the absence of light. Not something tangible.

"You're right," Ai said, her smile still illuminating her face, "but I hope you won't need luck again."

I had shooed Ai's paranoia away. At least until my accident the following month.

"I really fell asleep in the bathtub." I patted Ai's head as she sobbed, soaking my hospital gown. This was the second one I would have to change. "My internship at the hospital lasted forever. Then some drunks wouldn't leave the restaurant. I arrived home around midnight."

"And you felt like taking a bath?"

"I know it was late but—"

"I'm not talking about the time," Ai said in a childlike whimper. "You never lie in the bathtub."

"Well, now it's almost never."

Ai wailed. "It was because of me, right? I'm depressed all the time and that makes you stressed."

"Hey, no, no." I bowed my head in apology at the glaring nurses. For a moment, I wished I had drowned in the bathtub. "It makes me happy to cheer you up when you're down. To be there even after everyone else has left and nothing seems right."

Ai dabbed her tears with a tissue. The tides in her eyes had receded a bit. "Then because of Tokyo Medical University? It's so demanding it's killing you."

"Hard work makes me feel alive."

"I want you to feel like *staying* alive."

"Look, I'll make a plan to prevent accidents." I held Ai's milk-white hands on mine. "I'll avoid any dangerous situations and behaviors. To prove that I don't want to end my life. Deal?"

Ai's small mouth morphed into an upward-pointing crescent moon. "I'm starting to believe you."

After class the next day, I bought *okayu* gruel—I wanted to avoid choking on food—headed straight to my apartment, and ate dinner with my legs stuffed under my *kotatsu* table. When I was done, I went to freshen up. This time in the shower.

Once clean and still unscathed, I did the laundry and hung my clothes up to dry. This time in the bathroom.

Because of doing chores—and the scanty size of the gruel—my stomach groaned again. I tugged open the refrigerator. A relatively safe place; I'd never heard of anyone falling inside one and freezing to death.

The fridge only had a bottle of soy sauce and four eggs I'd kept for so long they could've hatched.

Should I go to 7-Eleven? No, it would increase my odds of being in a car accident, catching the flu, or getting hit by lightning.

Water was a better solution; I filled a glass from my four-gallon bottle. And another. And another. And another. Until my belly resembled that of a pregnant woman. At least I was no longer hungry like them.

Speaking of ladies, what if I called Ai? To tell her I had a safe and sound (and suicideless) day?

She phoned before I could.

"Are you okay?" No hello. Straight to the point.

"More than ever." I told her about my hazard avoidance plan and the

15

results.

"Great!" Ai chirped. "How about your ... mind?"

"My mind?" I sat at my comfy *kotatsu*. "I haven't given it much thought."

"So what are your thoughts now?"

I squinted at my half-empty glass of water before gulping it. "My mind is fine."

"Just ... fine?"

"I don't mind being just fine. "

Ai fell so silent, I couldn't hear her breathing. "Maybe I'm thinking too much. Oh, I'm being paranoid again, right?"

"No, no," I said. "Well, a tiny bit. But I don't mind that, either. It means you think about me. And that's one of the few things that makes me happy."

A weepy chuckle slipped from Ai's lips. "See? This is why I'm so scared of losing you."

"Don't be." I ambled to the four-gallon bottle and gulped down a glass of water. Talking on the phone always made me thirsty. "You'll never lose me. We'll be together till death do us part."

"Is that a marriage proposal?"

"More like a marriage innuendo," I said in a playful tone. "I'm not a fan of rushing to marry. I don't understand why some couples do that."

"Because they depend on each other for happiness?"

Ai was right. However, dependence wasn't. But if someone relied on you, was it fair to take away the bliss you gave them?

We said that couple's good night that lasts forever and hung up. Telephone calls made me hungry. Still, I refused to go out into the dangerous streets.

And so I drank more water. One, two, three glasses. Halfway through my fourteenth glass, my head started to boil. Until it became a sauna for my brain.

Falling on my knees, I flooded the floor with half-digested gruel and bile-flavored water.

This was my third time in Tokyo Medical University Hospital as a patient, and the seventh time Ai fished out a tissue from the breast pocket of her blouse.

"Who would have thought," I said, "that drinking water could kill you."

"You did think about it."

"I did?" I blinked at her.

"You study medicine." She buried her nose in her tissue. If she kept using it, it'd disintegrate in her hand. "You knew about water intoxication."

"I knew about it ... it just didn't cross my mind."

Ai hollered, her forehead pressed against my hospital gown. "I'm afraid to leave you alone. I think I'll move into your apartment."

"I like the idea," I began. "But are you sure it's a good one? My apartment isn't near Waseda University."

"It's all right. I'd rather take a thirty-minute subway ride every day than spend a lifetime without you."

I smiled. Ai's concern and devotion also made me want to spend my life with her. No, she was my life.

The next day, I helped Ai move her belongings from her house to mine. Skirts, shampoo, sanitary napkins. Little objects that hinted at a feminine presence in my apartment. I didn't mind. Because they had turned my house into a home. And especially because—

"Sure this is okay?" Ai asked as we lay naked and tangled under my *kotatsu*, only our heads peeking out of the blanket.

I contemplated moving, but if I did, I would knock over the glass of water on the table. Not that it would have bothered me much. "Guess it's too cramped to do it here."

"I'm not talking about that."

"Then ...?" I asked.

"I mean, me moving in here. Does it bother you? Maybe you want to do your things."

"Not at all." I kissed her slim, curled lips. "There are no things I want to do that don't include you."

"There must be some."

I pulled open my drawer of memories and rummaged inside. "Nope. Nothing."

"I think you've lost interest in daily activities? In life?"

"Listen," I said, knotting myself tighter around Ai's petite physique. "I enjoy it when we watch a movie at home instead of going to the cinema. When we cook meals we have no idea how to cook. When we are together in a room, studying for our exams, spooning inside the *kotatsu*, or just our sharing our everyday lives."

Ai pecked my lips then nestled herself under my arm. No, she wasn't only my life, but my lifeline.

One that I'd have to clutch with all my might in the following days.

"What?" I gripped my professor's lectern. "I didn't get the passing grade?"

She gave a half nod, half bow. "Sorry, but you've only attended class four times this semester."

"I've been in a few accidents."

"About that ..." My professor flicked her glasses back onto her nose. "Can I recommend a doctor to you?"

I scratched my disheveled hair. "I'm not hurt anymore."

"Maybe you have a wound—how to put it—that you can't see? But can feel?"

A sigh escaped me. "There's a rumor that my accidents weren't accidents.

But that's all it is. A rumor."

"Okay." My professor scribbled on a sticky note and slid it to me. "Call me whenever you want. We can talk about you retaking this class next semester. Or about anything you want to talk about."

I sighed again. Had no idea that one of the hardest things in life was to convince people that you didn't want to die.

As difficult as stopping a losing streak.

"What?" I spread my palms on my boss' desk. "I'm fired?"

"Lemme tell you, you're my best waiter, but customers can't wait. I need someone who can work at least four days a week. And you've been a bit unavailable lately."

"I really needed to take those sick leaves."

"About that, kiddo ..."

"It's all right. I understand, boss." I left before he could hand me his number with a you-can-call-me-anytime invitation.

That night I walked to my apartment with my head down. I had thrown into the trash not only my studies but also the ability to pay for them next year. Should I ask my parents for help? No, I would have to tell them about my serial accidents. And put up with a wanna-talk-about-it episode.

Better go straight home; I crossed the intersection, let the elevator take me to the 4th floor, and felt my way through the blackened hallway (the light bulb had died and hadn't been replaced since last week). It was so black it made me wonder if darkness was real. As real as a rope. Or a gun.

Or a window. Lit up by pale moonlight, it was the only visible object in the hallway.

What if I slid it open and repeated that deadly stunt? If I did, I wouldn't have to save up for my studies. Wouldn't have to find a temporary dead-end job. Wouldn't have to give my body and soul to a career that didn't fulfill me. Wouldn't have to survive, once I became a doctor, hours and hours of seeing people cry, bleed, or die.

Wouldn't have to live life.

Thinking about my life reminded me of Ai. Was she awake? Without turning on the light, I opened the door of my apartment and closed it in such a way not even a dog could have heard the sound.

Ai was sleeping sideways under the *kotatsu*. A common sight these days. She would prepare my favorite dishes: Salmon teriy*ai*ki, ra*i*men noodles, spaghetti a la monega*i*sque. And wait for me, often falling asleep.

If I jumped out of the window, Ai wouldn't have to feed me. Or fear that I would end my existence. She could start a brand-new, worry-free life.

But if I carried out my self-death sentence, Ai would become immensely sad—become someone without anyone to cheer her up. Make her smile, giggle, chuckle. And most scary of all, I wouldn't be able to share my life with her—watch movies with her, mess up the kitchen with her, share comfortable silences with her. That was worse than death.

I switched on the light.

"Look," I said to Ai, watching her eyes flutter open. "I made it here alive."

SEASON TO LOVE

My wife, Ayumi, expresses her feelings for me through her cooking.

I first tasted this behavior at our wedding. That day, possibly the happiest of our life, she arranged a whole tray of sushi—salmon, sea urchin, herring roe—to rival those served in fancy restaurants. It stirred me up. Who cooks right after exchanging marriage vows?

When upset, Ayumi's culinary choices became stingy. On one occasion, after we'd had an ugly fight, she gave me an apple with a fork stuck in it. She had eaten dinner first.

Wide-eyed, I asked her, "Is this a joke?"

"It's called a diet." Readjusting her sprouting bun, she sat across from me at the *kotatsu* table. We always pulled it out during winter to eat cozily in its futon.

"I only weigh seventy kilos."

"You're right." She bit the corner of her plump lip, her guilt-is-eating-me-alive gesture. "I'll make it up to you tomorrow. I promise."

Ayumi kept using this seasoned form of communication.

The time I surprised her with a gift at Christmas, she prepared a steamy *oden* pot—boiled eggs, fish cakes, soy-flavored broth.

The time I slept over at the house of a co-worker, Haru, Ayumi cooked rice—only rice.

The time she found out that Haru was short for the male name Haruki, and not Haruko, she made rice balls of various shapes—pandas, penguins, snowmen.

The most memorable time—memorable in a bad way—was when Ayumi stopped cooking altogether. For the first time in our two years of marriage.

"Takeout?" I blurted, gawking at the supermarket bento boxes sitting on the *kotatsu* table top.

"I was tired today. Had to shovel snow from the veranda." Ayumi picked a mushroom with her chopsticks and nibbled at it. "This is good."

I took a bite too. "Not as good as your cooking."

"Don't worry. I'll get back to it tomorrow."

The next day, she bought instant noodles at 7-Eleven. She told me she'd gone to a hot spring with her girlfriends, even though she was on her period.

The day after, Ayumi ordered a grilled shrimp pizza from Dominos. She explained she had menstrual cramps, even though her period had ended.

This went on and on for an entire week. One afternoon, watching Ayumi nap rosy-cheeked in the *kotatsu* futon, I chewed over the matter. She'd cooked to display her affection for me. Maybe that affection had cooled? Melted? Been thrown in the garbage like leftovers?

One Monday morning, I ate the red bean buns Ayumi had bought from across the street, waved goodbye to her, and walked to Tsukiji Station. Instead of forging ahead, I stood in the middle of its sloping steps, briefcase stiff in my hand.

I couldn't go to work. Not without asking Ayumi the big question. *Do you still love me?* Only five words, yet as hard to throw in the air as rocks.

But why interrogate her? She had acted like her usual self during breakfast. She chuckled at my dumb jokes, tossed out her cute remarks, listened to the thoughts no one else listened to.

Before realizing it, ten minutes had passed.

Then, as though summoned by my thoughts, Ayumi appeared, pacing along the street.

Without hesitation, I fished my mobile phone from my pocket and called in sick to work. Illness: food poisoning.

I waited for Ayumi to pass the station before trailing her, hiding behind parked trucks and scooters, a few meters back.

Where was she heading to? She wore her V-neck sweater, autumn-brown scarf, and knee-length skirt—the clothes she usually wore to cook and clean. And to go grocery shopping.

Had Ayumi gone out to buy dinner? She was heading to the place she frequented in the morning. Tsukiji Fish Market.

Hiding behind a tower of crab containers, I watched her approach a fish stall and examine the fresh products like a sushi chef.

She was planning to cook.

At last, Ayumi pointed to a fillet of tuna and handed two one-thousand-yen notes to the elderly man. Next, carrying the plastic bag, she plunged into the river of people. No exaggeration. I had to swim through them—finally getting carried away by the current.

Away from Ayumi.

21

I hunted for her among the throng until I couldn't walk anymore. But it didn't matter because she hadn't been up to anything weird. No, she'd decided to go back to being the usual Ayumi. The Ayumi whose heart always made it into my stomach. The Ayumi who, through my stomach, always made it to my heart.

Later that morning, I called the office and told them I was feeling better.

As soon as I arrived home, I was greeted by a distasteful surprise.

"McDonald's?" I stared at the Filet-o-Fish sandwich, French fries, and Coke.

"Not bad once in a while." Ayumi took a bite of the burger and dabbed the edges of her lips with a handkerchief. "Mm, that should be their slogan."

Feeling cold, I snuggled into the *kotatsu* futon. "You didn't buy anything else?"

"Something to drink, you mean?"

"Something to cook."

She giggled, holding her bun as if worried it would fall off. "Then I would have cooked it, silly."

I staggered to the refrigerator and hauled it open.

Empty. As it'd been for the past few days.

"You don't want McDonald's?" Ayumi tiptoed to my side. "Sorry. Want me to prepare instant noodles?"

"It's fine," I replied, still gaping at the chilly cavern in front of me. What did Ayumi do with the tuna? Hide it? Unlikely. It could only be preserved in the fridge.

Did that mean Ayumi had cooked the fish for lunch? No, she would have left some for me. Maybe she ate it with one of her girlfriends? That sounded likely.

Except Ayumi had lied about having bought the tuna.

Which only left one option: she shared it with someone she wanted to keep secret.

The more thoughts I fed to my theory, the stronger it became: Ayumi bought the takeout so she had a pretext to leave home, to go to the man's house. And she got rid of the garbage almost every day, to disguise that she'd invited him over for dinner.

To confirm all this, I could check Ayumi's mobile phone—no, I had a better plan.

But it would have to wait until morning.

"Are you going to cook dinner?" I asked Ayumi, stepping onto the frosty veranda.

"Dunno. I haven't felt inspired lately." She did her lip-biting habit. "Are you fed up with takeout?"

"Not really," I lied, though my reason for disliking it didn't have a pinch to do with the taste.

"Maybe I'll find my muse today," she said.

"I'm sure you'll find her. Or *him*." I flinched, wishing I could swallow back my words. At this pace, I would crush my scheme.

Ayumi seemed to have caught on to my distress, because, eyes cast down, she said, "Actually, motivation isn't the problem. It's just that—"

—*I'm not the one who motivates you*, I wanted to finish for her. No, I'd given her too many hints. Also, the words would not only sting Ayumi's ears, but also my own.

"Never mind." She released a resigned sigh. "I'll tell you at the right moment. Besides, it's about something ... you already know."

I goggled at her. So, she knew that I knew about the man? Perhaps she found out I'd followed her yesterday. Or smelled it in my demeanor.

Not wanting to disclose more information, I said goodbye to Ayumi and started toward Tsukiji Station. Like the previous day, I halted at the steps, called in sick to work, and stewed over the situation.

Funny. What hurt me the most wasn't that my wife had kissed or had sex with another man, but that she had cooked for him. Had invested her time and heart to fill his stomach. The thought nauseated me.

Funny. It pained me not that my wife had kissed or had sex with another man, but that she had cooked for him. Had invested her time and heart to fill his stomach. The thought nauseated me.

As I predicted, Ayumi left the house the same time as yesterday. With the same clothes. To the same place: the fish market. (She didn't glance back, so the theory that she'd seen me yesterday was debunked.)

On this occasion, Ayumi not only bought tuna, but also salmon, sea urchin, herring roe, seaweed sheets, and wasabi.

The ingredients of our wedding's sushi dish.

Once again, I failed to follow Ayumi—not because of the river of people, but the biting pain in my chest. A pain that immobilized me. Turned me into a vegetable.

Later that morning, I called to work again, to tell them that, although I still felt bad, I didn't feel like staying at home.

When I walked into the living room that evening, I found Ayumi at the *kotatsu,* her face buried in her hands, as though the Sushi Take-Out tray before her was a victim she had killed.

I settled myself in my seat, starving for answers. Answers that would surely leave a bitter taste.

"I have a confession to make," Ayumi uttered, still veiling her face. "I've been cooking these days. Or I should say, I never stopped cooking."

"I know," I said.

Ayumi removed her hands from her eyes, turned into crystals by tears. "Really?"

"I also have a confession to make—I've been spying on you."

She blinked confusedly at me. "Why?"

I told Ayumi everything. About me suspecting her, about me being right.

Instead of admitting her crime, she laughed, with such force her eyes flooded even more. "Silly, I'm not cooking for someone else."

My heart believed her, though not my mind. "How can I be sure of that?"

She pointed to the garbage bin under the kitchen sink. "You can check for yourself."

Blinking, I came out of the *kotatsu,* staggered to the trash can, and peeked inside. At the bottom, lay the crumbled remains of roe and urchin nigiri. The curled slices of salmon and tuna sashimi.

"But why?" I asked.

Ayumi gnawed at her lip so hard I thought it would bleed. "You told me I expressed my feelings to you with my cooking, remember?"

Right, I told her that a week ago.

The same day she'd stopped cooking.

"And you were right," Ayumi continued. "So I promised myself that I'd cook the best meal I could—but no matter how hard I tried, I could never make something that expressed how much I love you. In the end, I threw everything away and bought ready-made food."

Ayumi dropped her head, scattering her bun in all directions like the top of a palm. "I'm sorry. For having made you eat so badly."

Without a second thought, I dashed to the *kotatsu* and threw my arms around Ayumi. The Ayumi who had been so many things to me—my friend, my girlfriend, my wife. The Ayumi who had filled so many parts of me—my head, my stomach, my heart. The Ayumi who was more indispensable to me than food.

"It's all right," I whispered into her delicate ear.

Because this was the most delicious meal she'd cooked for me.

The most delicious one ever.

GRAVITY GIRL

When Chiyo opened her eyes that morning, she couldn't lift herself from the bed. *Oh god, what's happening?* She tried again but only managed to make her biceps sore, as if she'd been arm wrestling.

"Mom!" Chiyo shouted. Thank heavens her voice wasn't paralyzed. A minute passed, then another one.

Nobody came. Was her mother asleep, or was Chiyo having a nightmare?

Either way, she'd have to get out of this on her own. With gritted teeth and trembling muscles, Chiyo pushed herself up with her left elbow—pushed, pushed, pushed, finally succeeding. Progress! She did the same with the right one. Next, with the hardship of a last sit up, she angled forward until she rested on her backside, arms quivering and burning.

C'mon, c'mon.

Using her torso as her center of gravity, Chiyo spun ninety degrees and crawled off her bed, only to trip and stick to the floor like a starfish, rivulets of pain and sweat flooding her body.

"Chiyo?" her mother called out. "What's all that noise—oh, you fell out of bed? Are you okay?" When she reached Chiyo's side, she lifted her, but only a few inches.

Her mother laid Chiyo back to the floor. "Have you put on weight?"

"Mom, I'm very thin."

Her mother tried to help her up, only to crumble to the floor, panting. "I think we should call an ambulance. You need a doctor."

Two paramedics arrived twenty minutes later. With shaky muscles, the lanky one pulled Chiyo onto the stretcher, dark spots forming under the armpit area.

"Whoa, did you eat stones for breakfast?" he joked, which earned him a scold from his hefty partner.

Upon reaching Tokyo Medical University Hospital, Chiyo was hauled into a wheelchair and pushed by three nurses past hundreds of inquisitive eyes. Eyes that made her wish she could bury her head in the ground like an ostrich.

Fortunately, in no time, she got into the physician's office where he weighed her, checked her reflexes, and sent her to undergo a blood test.

"As I suspected," said the physician when Chiyo and her mother returned to his desk with the wheelchair. "She suffers from Major Mass Disorder. MMD for short."

"*Major Mass Disorder?*" Chiyo and her mother echoed simultaneously.

The doctor nodded. "Chiyo's cells are producing an excessive number of particles. In other words, they're increasing their weight."

"Without becoming fat?" her mother asked.

"This is because the particles are packed together. Think of a steel ball."

Chiyo's mother frowned, her pencil-thin eyebrows meeting in a point. "Shouldn't this make my daughter sick?"

"She *is* sick."

Chiyo slouched on her wheelchair, weighed down by the reality of the situation. "How did it happen?"

"The cause is not well understood." The physician pulled up his oversized pants. He also seemed to have a problem with gravity. "We only know that genetic and atmospheric factors play a major role. Somehow, they create an imbalance in the body's chemistry and physics."

"But you do have a cure, right?" Chiyo's mother twisted and untwisted the hem of her skirt.

"It's a newly discovered disease," the doctor said in an apologetic tone. "But we have an experimental treatment consisting of daily doses of *antimassants,* which will decrease the density of Chiyo's cells. With them, and exercise to strengthen her muscles, she'll be able to live a *relatively* normal life."

Chiyo's mother gave a nod to the doctor. Chiyo did the same, though the word "relatively" gave her a creeping sense of foreboding.

"Go, Grasshopper! Go!" Chiyo's classmates cheered her on both sides of the running track. Their voices, however, were muffled by the membrane of sweat blocking her ears—the result of the sizzling sun and her shooting adrenaline.

But mostly, the consequence of the colossal weight restricting her body. Dammit. She should have taken a heavier dose of antimassants.

Still, Chiyo—hiding her disease from her classmates and teachers—had insisted on entering the long jump championship.

"I'm Chiyo the Grasshopper," she muttered under her stifled breath. "I-I can't lose. I can't let my school down."

When the arbiter raised his hand, Chiyo propelled herself forward with her right foot and began to run. With each step, her feet squeezed her shoes, her arms fought the air. *C'mon, c'mon. Only five more steps.*

The instant her foot touched the takeoff board, Chiyo jumped, shooting her chest out, looking at a sky blurred by her sweat.

For the first time in a long time, she felt weightless. Like a leaf. This was the reason Chiyo had chosen this sport: to let her body abandon the ground and become one with the wind. Sure, only for a few seconds. But that fleetingness made the experience even more precious. Heavenly.

Chiyo landed with her arms and legs fully extended in front of her—and so hard, the sand exploded under her buttocks. Good thing it was a soft surface. If she had fallen on concrete, her hips would be in her lungs now.

The sand also helped to cushion Chiyo's head and back when she collapsed, run-down, without even being able to move her eyelids.

Anyhow, that didn't matter; she had accomplished her goal. But weird, why was everyone laughing? Because she looked as though she were stranded in the desert?

"I've seen snails jump farther than that," someone mocked from the crowd.

What? When Chiyo threw her head back, she saw the takeoff board a few centimeters from her eyes. *I only jumped in my mind.* She had turned from a grasshopper into a snail. As one, she would be stuck on the ground, without being able to touch the sky.

Perhaps forever.

Not being able to participate in her favorite sport devastated Chiyo. To cheer her up, her ex-teammates—who already knew about her physical disorder—invited her to the Shinjuku shopping area. They tried massage chairs in department stores, clothes in casual wear shops, donuts in extravagant coffeehouses.

By the time they reached Shinjuku Gyoen National Garden, Chiyo was already dragging her legs and swimming in sweat.

At last, conceding defeat to gravity, she crawled onto a bench under a cherry blossom tree and lay there, face up, her heart hammering in her head. Perhaps she should start taking her wheelchair out. Even if it made her look like a handicapped person. Well, in a sense she *was.*

Tsuki giggled. "You're so dramatic, Chiyo. We've only walked for an hour."

"Really?" Chiyo said, panting heavily. "It felt like a full-day marathon."

"Is it because of your disease?"

"Dunno." Mariko folded her arms across her chest. "Should we believe Chiyo?"

"Mariko!" Tsuki scolded.

"What if she's doing all this to attract attention?"

Tsuki's head hovered over Chiyo. "Is that true?"

In normal circumstances—meaning, when Chiyo was *normal*—she would have defended herself. Now she didn't even have the energy to move her tongue. Even if she could, would they understand the gravity of her situation?

"You see?" Mariko turned her back to the bench. "I've had enough of this." She waved them a cold goodbye.

"B-but we can't leave Chiyo here," Tsuki protested.

"Then carry her home."

Biting her plump lower lip, Tsuki knelt beside Chiyo, until their noses almost touched. "Sorry, I'm not strong enough to take you home. I'll call a taxi, okay?"

From that day on, Chiyo's classmates not only refused to hang out with her but also nicknamed her Gravity Girl, an American superheroine from the sixties. Unlike the fictional character, Chiyo didn't control gravity; gravity controlled her. And she wasn't a heroine, but a loser.

Chiyo had fallen to her lowest point in life.

"Come on." Chiyo's mother slumped onto Chiyo's bed and tugged at her planet-patterned pajamas. "You've been in bed all day."

Her head glued to the pillow, Chiyo said, "Why don't you try to lift me?"

Her mother let out a heavy sigh, aware of "Gravity Girl." She'd already filed a complaint with the school. "How about you find a summer job? To distract yourself?"

"Working as what? A paperweight?"

"I know you'll find something."

Actually, Chiyo *had* something to attend.

The last thing.

Chiyo had never written a suicide note before. She knew, though, to whom to address it.

Mom,

It's not your fault. My disease—I just can't carry the burden anymore. I wish I could save you from pain, but the truth is, I can't even save myself. Sorry. I know you'll never forgive me—I won't be able to forgive myself either.

Chiyo

After dropping the note on her bed, Chiyo slumped in her chair, panting. She'd been experiencing immense gravity lately—four times stronger than usual.

That would make her next movements feel as though they were being performed at the bottom of the sea. *It's okay.* This was the last time she'd have to make any physical effort.

Chiyo hauled herself into the elevator, fought the gravity generated by the ascent, and shoved open the door to the rooftop. Her muscles burned. Her skin dampened. But she couldn't give up her plan of giving up on life. Besides, she was only four steps away from the railing.

Go, Grasshopper! Go!

Chiyo took the first step. As soon as her foot touched the ground, a thousand needles stung her. But she bit back the pain and forged ahead.

When she took the second step, her other leg numbed.

The third step sent Chiyo falling to the concrete floor.

Her fourth step wasn't a step, but a crawl. Despite that, she managed to clutch the railing and—with all her might and remaining energy—pull herself up until she clung to the railing as if it were a sideways fireman's pole. She peeked down. The ant-sized cars triggered a fear of heights she didn't know she had.

Despite being terrified, Chiyo refused to back away. She didn't want to fight gravity anymore. Push, pull, plod. It was better to surrender to the forces of nature. Fall. True, the idea frightened her, but at least her heavy weight would drive her faster to the ground. Guaranteeing death.

Goodbye, world. Goodbye, gravity.

The next events passed in the darkness behind her eyelids. Chiyo let go of the barrier, leaned forward, and was shoved violently backward. She tumbled down, ending face up on the floor.

When Chiyo opened her eyes, she saw a hand holding hers. The owner had hair that made her want to comb it, eyes that resembled crescent moons, and a T-shirt that said NASA with the slogan "I need my space."

Not a very unusual sight—except the boy was fluttering above Chiyo like a flag.

Impossible.

"Hey, listen," the boy yelled, clutching Chiyo's hand. "Use your weight and pull me down."

"What?" Chiyo blurted. "Who are you? Where did you come from? Why are you floating?"

"Hurry up!"

With a short nod, Chiyo pulled the boy toward her, caught him in her arms, and rolled on the floor until she lay on top of his sturdy body. Wow, she *could* work as a paperweight after all.

"Please answer my questions now." Chiyo blushed since they were within kissing distance. It didn't help that the boy's hands rested on her back and the smell of his soap-scented skin tickled her nose.

"I'm Sora Harada," he began. "I was on the next building's rooftop. I saw you going over the railing and—"

"And you jumped to save me?"

"I didn't jump. I *floated*."

"Floated?" Chiyo blinked a few times.

"I was born with the ability to defy gravity. Or to put it in a scientific way, my cells have helium atoms inside them."

"Helium atoms?"

"What makes hot air balloons fly."

Chiyo turned over the implications of this statement. "Hey, you have the opposite of my condition."

"I know, I read about you in an online article," Sora said in a voice firm as steel. "That's why I was watching you."

"You mean *stalking* me."

"Sorry, but your mother wouldn't let me talk to you. Maybe she thought I was a reporter. And I couldn't meet you outside because you never go out." Sora pointed to the railing. "I know the reason now."

Chiyo winced. Why did a stranger have to be the first to know about her suicide attempt?

"I think you understand," she said, "how horrible it is to be oppressed by gravity."

"How about we discuss this in another place—preferably not on the floor."

"Sure ... but how do we stop you from floating into space?"

Sora extended his finger to the railing again. This time, Chiyo spotted, hanging on it, a black garment with brick-shaped bumps.

"A bulletproof vest?" she asked.

"A weight vest," Sora corrected. "I threw it here before saving you."

Chiyo nodded. The puzzle pieces were falling into place.

After that unconventional encounter, Chiyo met Sora almost every day. He made her feel light. So light she could engage in normal activities with him. Like going to the cinema.

They picked *The Martian,* a movie about a botanist-astronaut who became stranded on Mars. It reminded Chiyo of herself. Alone, helpless, stuck in a planet unsuitable for her. Unlike the main protagonist, though, she was on her own planet.

Chiyo tore her eyes away from the projection screen to look at Sora. *No, I'm not in a harsh habitat anymore. I'm safe.*

Perhaps sensing her gaze, Sora squinted at Chiyo, his eyes transforming into a skyline. "What's wrong? You don't like the movie?"

"Oh, no ... I like it a lot." She looked back to the projection screen, cheeks warming up. "You like it too?"

"I've already watched it eleven times."

"Wow, why?"

"I'll share something crazy with you." Sora rubbed the top of his untidy hair. "My dream is to work for NASA."

"Oh, that's cool—but why do you find that crazy?"

"Dunno, I think I'm setting the bar too high."

With a hesitant hand, Chiyo gripped Sora's arm. "You aren't. You can fly."

He stared at her as though he were seeing the universe in her eyes. After seeming to have come back to Earth, he flashed a sunny smile and said, "Thanks, I needed that."

Chiyo beamed back. Amazing. She had lifted someone's spirit instead of bringing it down. *I can do anything, like a heroine.* She could save people. Save herself. And most importantly, she could follow Sora anywhere. To the edge of the world.

Her theory turned on its head when Sora invited her to Yamanakako to stargaze, one of his favorite pastimes. At first, Chiyo hadn't had problems hiking up the hill. But as the minutes passed, she found it harder and harder to keep up with Sora.

No, I can't give up. Chiyo couldn't ruin this journey with Sora. Just a few more steps. Just a few—

With a last breath, Chiyo dropped onto a bed of pampas grass, facing the mantle of clouds that obscured the sky. Where were the stars?

Sora's slender eyes entered her field of vision, his hand cushioning the back of her head. "Chiyo, are you okay?"

"Keep going without me ..."

"No way," he said. "We're here so that *you* can see the stars, not me."

"I don't see any."

"They are there. We just need to get a bit higher."

"I'll drag you down." Chiyo would always be a boulder on people's shoulders. It had happened with her friends at school, and it was happening with her only remaining friend—perhaps throwing herself from the rooftop had been a good plan.

With the gentleness of handling a newborn baby, Sora laid Chiyo's head back on the grass, his warm touch replaced by the icy night air. Had he decided to leave her?

When she lifted her eyes, she saw Sora's crouched back, his arms offering a piggyback ride.

"Are you sure?" Chiyo blurted. "I'm a bit heavy ..."

"I might be lightweight, but I'm strong thanks to the exercise I get with my weight vests." Sora flexed his muscular arm, smiling brightly. "Also, if you cherish someone, that person is never a burden to you."

Chiyo gaped at him, her heart pounding hard. *So I'm important to him?* She no longer entertained the idea of leaving the world, because she belonged to someone's universe now. And not as a speck of dust, but as an entire planet.

Supporting her body on his back and hooking his arms under her knees, Sora carried Chiyo the rest of the way. Surprisingly, he did it as if she were as light as a feather, never complaining or faltering. That put her at ease, letting her focus on him and the feeling of his soft but solid back, the smell of his sunbathed hair, the sound of his shoes crackling invisible twigs.

After a while, though, the atmosphere became too silent. To break the auditory monotony, Chiyo asked, "Why do you want to show me the stars?"

"Because I *really* like them."

"Why is that?" She wished Sora had used the word "you" instead of "them." Wait, did that mean that her heart was slowly gravitating toward him?

"I like how distant and unreachable they are—even if you get onto a spacecraft and fly straight to the stars, you might never meet them. That's because their light takes millions of years to hit Earth. The light, in some cases, is from a dead star."

Chiyo looked up at the darkened sky. "Then it's better not to chase them."

"You think so? I still would." Sora lifted his head, joining her in her cloud watching. "Because it's something to look forward to. To light up your heart. To forget that you're walking in the dark. Sure, sometimes you'll discover that, that something doesn't exist. But so what? That light already helped you to get through the day. Survive."

"Something to look forward to," Chiyo repeated, searing the words in her mind. Looking down, she added, "I haven't seen the stars in a long time."

"You serious?"

"My condition doesn't let me climb to high places. It takes away my strength."

"You don't need strength now." Sora nodded toward the sky. "Just look up."

Chiyo followed his eyes to a dazzling spectacle. Stars of all shapes, sizes, shades. Some shone as bright as lighthouses. Some stretched on all sides like kites. Others formed glittering constellations including Pegasus, Virgo, and Sagittarius. *Maybe I don't have to jump to touch the sky.*

"B-but how?" she stuttered. "There wasn't a single star a few minutes ago."

"The chunk of clouds above us is gone."

Chiyo kept staring at the cosmic dust. "This is so great."

"You know what's greater?" Sora spun his head around and gazed into her eyes. "That we came to watch this together."

Her cheeks heated up so much she had to lean back to not to burn Sora's back. Was this the best moment to confess her new-found feelings to him? She was riding on his back under a starry sky. What else did she want? That all the planets aligned with each other?

"Sora?"

"Chiyo?"

Maybe Sora had feelings to confess too? Good timing. That way she wouldn't have to do it.

"You first," she said.

"All right. It's something that I've been wanting to share with you for a long time." With the same gentleness as before, Sora squatted down and let Chiyo hop off his back. Once face to face, he rested his firm hands on her shoulders. "I finally achieved my dream of being together—"

Chiyo gulped, her hope expanding like a balloon.

"—with the stars."

Her balloon popped. *"The stars?"*

Sora fished out an A4 paper from the pocket of his black chinos and handed it to Chiyo.

Congratulations, you've been accepted into NASA's Student Internship Program.

"We will provide you with a one-year student visa and airplane tickets to California," Chiyo read, word by word, to let their meaning sink in her brain. "Wait, this means you'll leave Japan."

"Unbelievable, right?" His eyes shone like starlight.

"Yeah, I can't ... believe it."

"What's wrong?" Sora asked, seeming to detect the cloudiness in Chiyo's eyes.

His lifelong dream had become real. She should be happy for him, but couldn't be; she wanted him to keep his feet on the ground. However, did she really want to cut his new wings?

"Nothing." Chiyo stepped forward and hugged Sora so he wouldn't see her tears. "Wow, congratulations. I bet you worked hard."

"Not really," he admitted. "I just mentioned my condition to the NASA people. Maybe they are interested in my experience with zero gravity."

"I'm sure you'll do well."

Sora nodded, then added, "So what did you want to tell me?"

"Never mind." Chiyo pulled away with a smile, her hands still on Sora's back. "It's nothing important."

He drew back too. "Are you crying?"

She dug out a tissue from her jean's pocket and blew her nose into it. "I'm just happy for you."

Sora scratched his unruly hair. "Sure it's not because we'll be far away from each other? If that's the case, I—"

"Hey, bring me a star when you come back, okay?" Chiyo interrupted. "You said they were unreachable, but I think you can catch one. You're the kind of person who can turn anything into reality. Turn everything down, up."

Sora stared at Chiyo for a few seconds—seconds that felt like light years. At last, with a radiant eye smile, he said, "Okay, I promise."

Sora's last months in Japan passed at the speed of light. Why did happy moments move faster than unhappy ones? Whoever created time got the whole thing switched around.

And so the day arrived when Chiyo had to see Sora depart. She did it at a terminal, gripping his NASA T-shirt, with the massive heaviness she thought would never show up again.

"Are you going to be okay here on Earth?" Sora asked.

Chiyo lowered her face to the floor. "Maybe just a little *down.*"

"Don't be." Gently, he lifted her face by the chin. "Remember, I'll bring a star for you."

Gravity had made it hard for Chiyo to curl up her lips today. But now, she managed to do so. "Okay, I'll be waiting for you."

Sora smiled back, a smile that lost its momentum at the end. "You know, Chiyo, I've also been wanting to tell you some—"

Before he could finish, an echoing voice announced, "Flight AA11 is now boarding, all passengers please proceed to the gate."

"You're going to miss your plane," Chiyo said. "Tell me by phone or text."

"All right." Sora wrapped his arms around Chiyo, pressing his weight vest against her chest. "Goodbye, Gravity Girl."

Chiyo hugged him back, tears flooding her eyes. "Goodbye, Astro Boy."

Waving vigorously at her, Sora joined the line of voyagers, glided through security, and vanished behind a dim, metallic wall.

From the terminal's waiting room, Chiyo watched the airplane take off and soar through the cloudless sky, getting tinier and tinier until it became a dot on the horizon. Flickering, unreachable, like a star. True, she wouldn't be able to reach it even if she could fly like Sora. But it didn't matter. Because she had something to look forward to. And who knew—

"Maybe if I keep Sora in my heart," Chiyo whispered to herself, "one day I'll get as high in the sky as him."

THE CLERK NAMED HANDA

The most anticipated part of my day is drawing near—buying my midnight snacks at 7-Eleven. The excitement doesn't come from the snacks, though.

It takes me around two minutes to arrive at the 7-Eleven, which is close to the gloves manufacturer I work for. As soon as the automatic sliding door swishes open, I'm greeted by a heavenly blast of air conditioning. After scanning the shelves thoroughly, I drop into my shopping basket a mayonnaise tuna rice ball, a cup of "Chili Tomato" instant noodles, and a can of Asahi Super Dry beer.

With the first part of my task done, I stride to the cashier counter—drowning in anxiety, because this next feat is like diving into a pool; no matter how many times I jump into the water, I know I will be cold all over again.

"Welcome, sir," greets the clerk, Handa as shown on her name tag, bowing her head fifteen degrees. Her politeness isn't her only asset, though. It's also her slick hair, which cascades down her shoulder; her nose, which is slender and upturned; her ample lips, which have left me drooling more than any gourmet dish does; and her bust, which is just right, neither too voluptuous nor too modest.

I watch The Clerk Named Handa while she scans my food items and tucks them into a plastic bag. More specifically, I observe her fingers, which are twig-thin, fast-paced, and porcelain-white. No doubt, the hands of a woman are a wonder of nature. They are the perfect balance between fragility and tenacity, purity and sensuality, especially the ones belonging to the nymph before me.

"That will be 510 yen, please," says The Clerk Named Handa with her soft, breezy voice, summoning me back to my awareness.

With a short nod, and without daring to confront her eyes, I get out my wallet, gather the amount showing in the cash register, and give it to her shakily. I might as well be returning a stolen item.

Then the miracle happens.

When The Clerk Named Handa takes the money I'm passing to her, her thumb, index, and middle finger brush my palm for one, two, three seconds. They are soft like a nightgown made of pure silk. Humid like the air after a summer rain. Warm like a blanket that has been sunbathing the whole afternoon. I try my hardest to sear this sensation in my mind. But as usual, it fades into the recent past, because memory alone can't do justice to the real thing. Perhaps it's for the best. It'll hurt me to have this unforgettable feeling just as a second-hand experience, anyway.

"Thank you, sir," The Clerk Named Handa says, setting time into motion. She ends the task with a forty-five-degree bow.

I return her gesture with a short nod. And a hidden smile—because she made my day tonight.

After work this Tuesday, I go back to the 7-Eleven and gather my daily midnight snack: turnip wasabi rice ball, a cup of miso soup, and a bottle of Budweiser. After that, I amble to The Clerk Named Handa.

"Welcome, sir," she chirps with a perfectly angled bow.

As she receives my notes, her finely sculpted fingers kiss my palm. Tonight, they share the same dampness and tepidness of a hot towel. That glow follows me to my apartment—and stays with me until I drift cozily into sleep.

This Wednesday, I pick a minced chicken rice ball, a bag of squid crackers, and a Kirin canned cocktail before sauntering to the counter. Tonight, the fingers of The Clerk Named Handa are as chilly and wet as seashells after being washed by the surf. Especially wet. Did she just wash her hands?

That theory shatters when I lift my head and spot tears glossing her obsidian eyes. Seeing that I'm looking at her, she hastily wipes them with the back of her hand and offers a bow.

"Thank you ... sir," she says in a brittle voice.

As I exit the sliding doors, a swarm of questions swirl in my head. What hardship could be weighing on the mind of The Clerk Named Handa? Heartbreak? Headache? Homesickness? And most importantly, why did she have to sponge her tears with her own hands? Why wasn't there anyone around to assist her?

I wouldn't have hesitated to use my hands. Okay, perhaps I would have. Not only because I'm a man, an adult, a stranger—but also a coward. I would probably have tucked my hands in my pocket and walked out of the convenience store.

Like I'm doing now.

Thursday night, I quickly collect my snacks—*kombu* seaweed rice ball, a carton of low-fat milk, a can of Yebisu beer—and step in front of The Clerk Named Handa. To my great relief, her fingers are dry this time, drier than the discarded armature of a cicada. Wait, perhaps that isn't a good sign.

When I peek up, plump lips made thin by a smile blow away my worries.

"Thank you, sir," she says in a melodious, almost sing-song voice.

"Thank you," I echo, returning her grin.

On my way back to my apartment, a realization strikes me like a misdirected baseball—this is the first time I've exchanged words with The Clerk Named Handa. I bring my hand to my mouth, ashamed of being proud of such an insignificant achievement.

Like every Friday—or rather, every day—I undergo my routine and buy my midnight snacks: miso paste rice ball, a cheese and egg sandwich, and a can of Sapporo beer.

Then something special happens.

While The Clerk Named Handa picks up the coins from my hand, her fingers linger on my skin longer than usual. Brushing it, tickling it, warming it. For one, two, three, four, five seconds! The astonishment is so strong, I saunter out of the 7-Eleven without remembering the seconds after this incredible event.

Wait a minute, perhaps I'm seeing colors where they aren't, like a reverse version of color blindness? Perhaps The Clerk Named Handa found it difficult to collect all the coins I'd produced? Perhaps she was worn-out or absent-minded? Perhaps I counted more seconds than actually passed?

No, I'm not deluding myself. She clearly touched my palm for a prolonged time. That's as certain as yesterday's candid smile and the cordial *Thank you, sir.*

I'm sure of myself now.

And what to do next.

On Monday, while hunting for tonight's snacks (a *kishu* plum rice ball, a can of black coffee, a bottle of unfiltered sake), I prepare myself for my move. The plan is this: while handing my cash to The Clerk Named Handa, I'll hold her fingers with mine—as if I were readying myself to kiss her hand—and examine her reaction. True, it's not the most audacious display of chivalry. But something is better than nothing. Plus, I have nothing to lose.

After pretending to check some shelves, to buy myself some time to harvest enough courage, I march toward the cashier counter. Toward my greatest fear and joy. Toward my main source of hope and despair.

Toward The Clerk Named ... Sada.

I stand there gawking at this woman with narrow, downcast eyes; black hair tied into an updo; bangs right above her eyebrows.

I'm left speechless, so she's the one who shatters the silence.

"Excuse me, may I help you?" she asks raising her skittish eyes.

I shoot her a nod. "Do you know what happened to The Clerk Named Handa?"

She bows in a weird, sideways angle. "I'm sorry, but I'm new here. I don't know the rest of the staff."

"You haven't seen another female clerk here?"

"I'm afraid not."

"And no one has told you anything about her?"

"Nothing at all."

"Okay, thank you for the information." I spin around and put my purchased goods back into their respective shelves—since, for the first time ever, I'm not in the mood for my daily midnight snack.

Tuesday: I immediately rush to the 7-Eleven after work. I have two theories: The Clerk Named Handa caught the flu, so the manager hired someone to temporarily replace her, or The Clerk Named Handa found it too stressful to work every day, so she cut back on her shifts.

"Or maybe she quit," I whisper to myself while my eyes remain glued to The Clerk Named Sada, who blinks at me with a question mark on her face.

Worried about being mistaken for a weirdo, I look down and sulk out of the convenience store. This would be my second day without my midnight snacks.

Friday: due to an abstinence-driven urge for my daily midnight snack, I visit the 7-Eleven, grab a salmon roe rice ball, a 100% orange juice, a bottle of Suntory whisky, and swing them into my shopping basket. At the cashier counter, I catch sight of ... The Clerk Named Sada.

I pass her my food and drinks, pay, and carry them out of the 7-Eleven in a plastic bag, muttering to myself, *Winners know when to quit,* although I've never believed that myself.

Still, that's what I do tonight.

And probably from now on.

This Saturday, instead of going to the 7-Eleven, I take a solitary trip via train to a sushi bar in Ginza. Not only because I'm sick of eating rice balls from convenience stores, or because buying my midnight snacks has become tasteless without The Clerk Named Handa, but also because I enjoy watching sushi chefs handcraft their edible art. The minimalist salmon sashimi, the stylish eel nigiri, the elegant avocado *temaki,* the chromatic beetroot and tuna *uramaki.*

The departure of the train shakes me out of my epicurean reverie. Rapidly, I stretch my arm to grip a grab handle. Odd. Why is it soft and smooth and sweaty and—

When I face to my left, I discover that someone's right hand has already clutched the handle. My gaze travels from the person's blouse sleeve, to her pale shoulder blades, to her swan-like neck, and finally to her face. Her silky dark hair, her fleshy full lips, her shapely onyx eyes. Those eyes stare at me as though I were an old but cherished photo. And like one, we stay frozen in place, with our hands exchanging heat. And hope—at least for me.

"Hello, sir," she greets with a two-degree bow, a smile parting her lips.

"Hello," I parrot poorly.

A miracle has happened.

HERBIVORE MAN

I'm a herbivore man. That doesn't mean I stay away from animal meat, but from women's. And no, I'm not shy, ugly, or gay. I simply detest the idea of becoming the shopping accessory for a girlfriend or the automated salaryman of a wife.

My life as a herbivore man is sup*herb*. I wake up in the afternoon and go to my part-time job at Deer's Diner. After work, I eat ramen noodles or curry rice at a restaurant. In the evening, I drink beer or sake in an izakaya. At night, I stay home to watch anime, read manga, and—more times than I'd like to admit—engage in visually-aided self-gratification.

I enjoy this life, especially now that I share it with Katsura, a carnivore woman.

I first bumped into Katsura at Deer's Diner, when I brought a veggie burger to her table.

"Did you know"—she pointed at Rina, the waitress with the heaviest makeup—"that some lipsticks are made with cow brains?" Katsura's lips were blood-red, probably the result of cow-brain-free cosmetics.

I scratched the back of my head. "Sorry, I must've skipped that class."

"Your boss should have taught you that," she said. "You work in a vegan restaurant."

The food business had three types of customers: those who ate with their mouths shut, those who ate without shutting their mouths, and those who didn't eat or shut their mouths. Katsura belonged to the third category.

But I knew how to deal with her. "I apologize on behalf of my co-worker." I offered her a forty-five-degree bow. "And I'll make sure she buys brainless lipsticks."

Katsura squinted at me as if I were a glowing jewel. "You're really nice to women, aren't you?"

"To customers in general," I replied.

"You were colder with the foreigner. You know, the one who complained that his vegetarian meatballs weren't hot enough."

She was spot on: I treated women nicely—to avoid drama with them as much as possible. Nothing upsets me more than a squealing, sobbing, or shrieking woman.

"I like men who are nice to women." Katsura rested her elbow on the table and her chin on her fist. "How 'bout you join me for dinner?"

I gawked at her. "Y-you're asking a waiter to eat with you?"

"What's the problem? Waiters eat too, right?"

"But it's crazy ..."

"It's fine," my beefy boss said as he wiped the table next to us. "You're thirty and haven't dated anyone in two years. Time to set roots!"

I scowled at my boss, then at Katsura, who smiled so broadly I worried her head would split in half.

In the end, I joined her for dinner, telling myself, *She'll get fed up of me soon.*

I would eat my own words.

The next day, Katsura invited me—or rather, forced me—to go watch Wonder Woman in the cinema with her. I didn't like the plan since I had no intention of having a girlfriend, even one as good-looking as Katsura.

So I did my best to avoid romantic situations. Like not sharing the popcorn that she'd bought (she insisted that one big bag had more popcorn than two small ones), or sipping from her straw (she assured me that the Coke tasted better than any she'd drank before), or going to my apartment (she begged me to watch my collection of harem anime together).

"Listen." I dodged Katsura's kissing attempts, a difficult feat when you were pinned against the wall of a park toilet. "Don't you think you're being a little, uh, *assertive?*"

"You have a problem with that?" She relaxed her grip on my wrists. "Oh, you believe women should be passive, right?"

"Not at all. It's just, this is the first time I've met—"

"A carnivore woman." Katsura smirked, licking her reddish lips.

"I thought you were a vegan."

"I don't eat animal meat, but I eat *men's.*"

"You're a cannibal?" The possibility made me want to run away. Or throw up. But I didn't dare to move with Katsura's knee under my crotch.

"No, silly." She got so close I could smell the French wine she'd drunk at the park bench. "I'm a *carnivore woman.* You know, a response to herbivore men. They've been inside their pen for too long. We women are hungry." She widened her already large eyes. "Oh, don't tell me that you're—"

I nodded. "I'm a herbivore man. I've been trying to tell you, but you haven't given me the time. Or space."

"I'm sorry." Katsura pulled away from me, freeing my crotch from danger. With a ninety-degree bow, she added, "And don't worry, I understand."

I gaped at this vegan carnivore woman. That'd been a 180-degree transformation.

Did I stop being her prey?

I was stacking plates on a table when someone tapped me on the shoulder. I swiveled around.

Katsura.

She was wearing her temple-to-temple smile—not only that, also a pink dress she could've stolen from a life-size doll, a purple ribbon tied to look like rabbit ears, and crystal slippers that resembled Cinderella's.

"Ready for our date?" Katsura tilted her head to the side.

"N-no, because I don't remember us having one."

"You have such a bad memory." She giggled, cupping her mouth.

I grew wary of the plan Katsura was cooking. "Sorry, but I'm working."

"You can finish earlier today." My boss popped up over my shoulder. "To go to the firework festival with such a beautiful lady."

"A-are you sure, boss?" I'd been so out of touch with the outside world, I'd forgotten summer had arrived. I turned my attention to Katsura. "Don't tell me we're going there."

She straightened her head and gave it a short shake. "It'll be romantic, don't you think?"

I gulped. Hopefully not.

"Shouldn't you have worn a yukata?" I asked Katsura as we walked alongside the wall of a high school.

"This dress is cuter than a casual kimono." She did a ballerina spin.

"It doesn't suit you—same with this girly behavior. It's not very you."

She gave me a kitten grin. "I am whatever I wanna be." Before I could make an ungraceful retreat, she stopped in her tracks. "Here we are."

On my left stood a pillar with a bronze nameplate that read "Tokyo Metropolitan Shinjuku High School."

I took a few steps back. "I thought we were going to see the fireworks."

"We will." Katsura, to my amazement, clutched the metal fence and flung herself over the top. Was she a cat? She extended her arms toward the sky. "Your turn. And don't worry, I'll catch you."

"Sure no one's gonna catch *us*?"

"It's all right. I'm allowed in. I used to study here."

I nodded, as if her words made perfect sense. No, I had to escape, even if that made me look unmanly.

But if I abandoned Katsura, she'd have to watch the fireworks alone in the dark. Whatever. She deserved it. For disturbing me at work and for not understanding that for men, no means no.

"For a minute, I thought you'd run away." Katsura climbed yet another fence, not as high as the previous one.

I sighed. "No way. I'm a gentleman."

On the other side of the fence was a swimming pool. The water shone a deep shade of blue, with the crescent moon casting silver ripples on it.

"Cool," I said. "But why did you pick this place?"

"I read this manga where a boy and a girl watch fireworks at a pool." Katsura wrapped herself on my arm, almost toppling us into the pool. "I found the scene romantic, so I've been wanting to copy it with someone."

"But why does it have to be me?"

Katsura locked her huge eyes on me. "Isn't it obvious? Because I'm falling in love with—" Before she could finish her sentence, she slipped and dragged me into the pool with her. I floated in a world of bubbles. When I emerged, I spotted Katsura flailing in the water like an ex-high school girl who'd skipped swimming class.

As I was trying to pull her to firm land, a blast rippled through the pool. I gazed up. The sky had turned red and stars were falling to the earth. The apocalypse? No, the fireworks display had started.

Bad timing.

Has Katsura given up on me? I wondered while I drank a latte at my tea table. Possibly. Her operation "Eat the Herbivore Man" had hit rock bottom yesterday.

And resurfaced today.

A ding of the bell sent me to the front door. I pulled it open. Before me stood Katsura, wearing a white blouse, a gray scarf, and a skirt so long she could walk and sweep the floor. Did she get these clothes from her mother's closet?

"H-how do you know where I live?" I stuttered.

Katsura grinned. "Your boss gave your address to your beautiful girlfriend."

I released a sigh, marking a mental note to find another job as soon as possible. "Okay, what are you doing here?"

Still smiling, Katsura lifted two plastic bags full of food. "To cook for you, darling." Without my approval, she took off her pumps and barged into my apartment. I didn't like the smell of this.

My mind changed when she began cooking, filling the air with the sweet scent of carrots, onions, sake, and soy sauce.

"What are you preparing?" I asked, peering over Katsura's shoulder.

She was using my electric cooker and tea table since my apartment lacked a kitchen. "Vegetable soup."

"Forgot to tell you. I'm not a vegan. I just happen to work in a vegan restaurant."

"What?" Katsura spun around. "You're a meat-eater herbivore man?"

I offered a firm nod, hoping the revelation would drive her away from me.

"It's all right." She faced the rising steam again. "You learned how to stop eating women. I'm sure you can do the same with animals."

Giving up, I sat cross-legged on the floor and watched Katsura's profile, sleeves rolled up, hair tied into a tight bun, lips sipping from a small plate now and then. This was how it felt to have a wife? Uh, not as bad as I'd thought.

"Don't just sit there," she scolded. "Get the bowls and chopsticks!"

"Okay, okay." I stepped to my plastic storage cabinet, took out the items Katsura had requested, and slumped across from her.

We ate in a tight-lipped, husband-and-wife fashion. The vegetarian soup tasted pleasant. Like home.

"So how was your day, honey?" she asked, reverting to her sweet self.

"Not so good," I replied. "I forgot to buy groceries, I found out I have a cavity, and now I have an intruder in my apartment."

"This intruder must be really cute. That's why you don't mind."

"Actually, I do." I put down my chopsticks. "Besides, you're not *that* cute." My words were horrible. But how else to stop her dumb game?

"You're so mean." Katsura's stroked her cheeks as if to make sure she still had a face. "But what do you mean?"

"Your eyes are too big, your lips too red, and your skin—its' like it's made of porcelain."

"Even *that* is too good for you." She dropped her chopsticks on the table and rose up. "Look at you, you're thirty and still don't have a wife, kids, or a decent job."

"Then leave this loser. The door is wide enough for you."

Katsura's eyes filled with tears. Boiling ones. "*You* get out!" She darted to the bathroom and slammed the door behind her.

With an aching heart and itchy nerves, I followed her path and twisted the doorknob. Locked. "I'm sorry. You okay?"

"We're done," she shouted, her voice muffled by the wall of wood separating us. "I want a divorce!"

I sat with my back leaning against the door. Mental note: never admit a woman into your apartment again.

"You still there?" A voice pulled me back from my dreamless sleep. Katsura.

Rubbing my eyes, I staggered up and, with my lips brushing the door, asked, "You're not going to give me the cold shoulder anymore?"

"I'm not cold. But *hot*."

"That happens sometimes. Turn the shower off and on again."

"I'm not showering," Katsura teased in a sultry voice. "I'm waiting for you. Naked."

I became stiff at the speed of light. "Y-y-you're joking, right?"

"Come and see by yourself. I unlocked the door."

The bulge in my shorts became harder and harder, until it hurt. No, I had to resist this final test.

"I'm sitting on the toilet," Katsura said. "If my legs were the hands of a clock, they'd be pointing to five past eleven."

Patience, persistence, perseverance.

"Now to ten past ten."

Assurance, autonomy, abstinence.

"Quarter to nine. Aaah!"

Serenity, self-confidence—screw it.

I burst into the bathroom. Katsura was naked indeed.

On the dirty floor.

"Katsura!" I grabbed the towel and draped it around her pale body. She must've fallen while performing her stripping show. Blushing, and pinning my little friend between my legs, I checked her body for bruises or bleeding. Thank heavens. She didn't have any.

But now I had an unconscious naked woman in my apartment.

"What happened?" Katsura rubbed her eyes, then her temples. "I got food poisoning? You gave me meat?"

"No, but you wanted to show me yours." To keep from seeing her bare body—and developing mating impulses—I'd dressed her in my "Save Water, Shower With Me" T-shirt and my cleanest shorts.

"Oh, I remember." She slumped back on my bed, her arm shielding her eyes from the ceiling lamp. "I wish I didn't. It's too embarrassing."

"So why did you do it?"

"I told you, because I'm falling—you know what, never mind." Katsura buried herself in the blanket. "I give up. I'll become a herbivore woman."

"Good," I said, a little too weakly. "It's not that bad once you get used to it. Actually, it's sup*herb*."

"Really?" She poked her head out of the blanket. "What's so great about it?"

"You get to eat alone, drink alone, and become better at being alone."

"That sounds a bit—lonely."

"True." I ambled to my desk and switched on my TV-sized computer screen. "But I get plenty of time to watch this." I scrolled through my sacred anime selection.

"Lemme see." Katsura rose from the bed and leaned to the screen. She seemed to be a real fan of films without real people. "Oh, you have Tokyo Ghoul. I've been planning to watch it."

My eyes enlarged. "You're a member of the human race and you've never watched Tokyo Ghoul?"

Katsura scratched the back of her head. "I've been busy preying on men."

"You're not doing it anymore. Wanna watch the anime now?"

"Sure." She stretched my T-shirt lengthwise. "But can you give me something else? I look like a potato sack with this."

"Sure," I replied. "I have a smaller one, but it's a bit childish. It says, 'No Drama Llama.'"

"Childish? No, *adorable!*"

After buying rice crackers and a bottle of French wine from the 7-eleven, we watched the anime sitting on the bed. But I couldn't focus on it. My eyes kept stealing glances at Katsura, the girl who liked me and became like me. Who lent me her loneliness to accompany mine. Who gifted me foolish memories that'd make me chuckle alone in the future.

"What's wrong?" Katsura asked me, noticing my straying eyes. "You don't like the anime?"

"No, I like it a lot," I said, without unlocking my eyes from hers. "Actually, I fell in love with it."

ODD ICHIKO

Ichiko, like a good accountant—or rather, an obsessive one—counts everything.

On February 10th, she counted the times she had physical contact with people. When ...

... her fingers stroked the palm of a FamilyMart clerk as she paid for her breakfast.

... she squeezed her way into the subway train in the morning rush hour. A schoolgirl bumped her head against Ichiko's chest. A housewife grazed Ichiko's arm with her breast. A salaryman accidentally—at least she wanted to think so—brushed her buttocks with the back of his hand.

... she gave a last-minute tax return to her manager.

... she got the same tax return back with a one-hour scold.

... her palm felt the fingers of a 7-Eleven clerk while paying for her lunch.

... her co-worker Nishikata, despite her previous death threats against him, rested his hand on her shoulder.

... she shoved her way into the subway train in the evening rush hour. Since inside was a jumble of humanity, Ichiko found it impossible to tell how many people had made physical contact with her (or how). So she just counted the parts of her body receiving foreign warmth.

... she had physical contact with yet another clerk while paying for the KFC she'd have for dinner.

... she touched—perhaps for too long—the hand of a handsome man who handed her a flyer.

The final result was 14 times.

On February 12th, Ichiko counted every breath she took, starting with her first exhalation in the morning, then moving on to those she expelled doing the following activities:

Brushing her teeth, washing her face, and tying her hair into a ponytail.

Putting on her office clothes and light makeup.

Trotting from her home to the station.

Buying and eating breakfast.

Arriving at work.

Working.

By the time Ichiko left her workplace, she was short of air and longing for a break. (She wouldn't be like this if she had counted with her head instead of her mouth.)

But if she quit, she would never find out how many times she breathed per day—wait, there was another way. With what scanty energy remained, Ichiko pulled out her iPhone from her handbag and typed on Google "How many breaths does a person take in a day?" She scrolled down until spotting the average, which took into account some moderate exercise: 17,000-30,000.

February 13th.

Since today's date was a prime number—therefore, a special one—Ichiko decided to deviate from her routine: instead of counting an activity she executed throughout the day, she would count one she'd done ever since she was conscious.

With this idea still fresh in her mind, after work, she dipped into a Starbucks, ordered a double espresso, and plopped down on a stool with a window view (a habit she developed when she used to count passersby). But what to count? While checking her lipstick in her glassy reflection, the answer struck her.

How about the times she had laughed?

Taking another sip of espresso, she set her analytical brain to work. However, she couldn't for the life of her remember when she had ever laughed.

Oh, yes! When Nishikata—nah, that time was more annoying than amusing.

That's right. The time her friends—wait, she didn't have any.

Aha! That day her dog, Bone—no, he died before he could do anything silly.

A balloon of air swelled in Ichiko's throat, finally blowing out of her mouth as laughter. How funny. She'd been alive for twenty-four years and six months, and she had never laughed—this was her first time. Or was she crying? Perhaps both.

Speaking of crying, how many times had she done it? Counting this would be easier.

When Bone was run over by that Mazda3. (1 time.)

After Ichiko broke up with Hisanori. (4 times.)

After Daishi broke up with her. (3 times.)

After Goro left her for her sister. (2 times.)
While attending her sister's wedding—hers and Goro's. (4 times.)
That evening she watched the movie One Litre of Tears. (10 times.)
Wiping tears provoked by opening old wounds, Ichiko made the final mental calculations.

Times she'd laughed: 1
Times she'd cried: 25.

February 14th.
Ichiko visited the Starbucks again to repeat yesterday's feat.
But what should she count this time? Ichiko glanced around the establishment, hunting for ideas. When she spotted a poster advertising a Valentine's Day special chocolate drink, one bubbled up in her head.
How many kisses had she ever given or gotten? Taking two sips of her double espresso, she plunged into her memories.
Her 1st kiss—or rather, indirect kiss—was in high school. During lunch break, she leaned against her crush's desk, then sipped her 7-Up and offered him some from the same straw. He said very naturally, "Okay, thanks," and drank.
Her 2nd kiss was in university. While wandering the streets alone one Christmas—at the time she had neither friends nor boyfriend, pretty much like the present—she stumbled upon a foreigner, who introduced himself as a YouTuber from Montenegro. That day, he was doing the "Kiss or Slap" challenge, where people choose either to kiss or slap him. In the end, Ichiko picked kiss. (1) because she was alone on Christmas, and (2) because she was alone on Christmas.
Her 3rd happened three years ago when she went alone to a club in Shinjuku. One, two, three, four glasses of vodka later she was listening to an unknown song, dancing unknown steps, and kissing unknown lips. She neither regretted nor relished the experience—because it'd been tasteless. Meaningless.
The 4th (and first with an animal) was with Bone.
The 5th was with Hisanori. Ichiko couldn't remember their first kiss (the freshness of kissing had already dissipated from her life). However, she could roughly recall how many times they had kissed.
In their first month together, they did it an average of 5 times a day. In the second, that number declined to 3. In the third, it descended to 1. On the third month, it dropped to 0—because they had become a divided couple. Mentally and physically.
Gulping her caffeinated fuel, she made the math ... she'd shared approximately 270 kisses with Hisanori. Adding the previous ones, made it 275.
The same negative kissing trend had repeated with Daishi and Goro (she

couldn't make out why). But with a couple of differences: her relationship lasted two months with the former and two weeks with the latter.

Ichiko tapped her temple. She'd kissed Daishi 240 times and Goro 70 times. That plus all the past kisses would give her the ultimate sum: 585 kisses.

Since kissing was the prelude to lovemaking, why not count the times she had engaged in it? That would be easy, since she'd only had sex with boyfriends, starting with Hisanori.

Her first night with him was two years ago at his apartment. He had invited her there with the excuse of not being able to bring his dog out.

"Sorry, but Tengo goes crazy when he sees a cat," he told her, "like a goat in mating season—come to think of it, he may have a thing for cats."

To which Ichiko replied, "Okay, let's sleep together." True, Hisanori was trying to trick her, but she couldn't fool herself anymore. If she didn't become more proactive—or provocative—she would reach her thirties single and still a virgin.

With this in mind, or rather hoping she hadn't lost her mind, she followed Hisanori home and made love with him on his futon. Then again in the shower. Then on the futon again. 3 times.

The number three became a common sight in their sex life. After officially being together, they made love 3 times a week, and always using 3 positions: one up, table for two, and sixty-nine. This pattern repeated throughout their three-month relationship (for some reason, without decreasing in number like in the case of the kisses).

Next was Daishi, who'd been a rabbit. He even moved in with Ichiko so they could do it every day. And they did. Once after dinner at 8 p.m. Another time before sleeping at 10 p.m. Another time half asleep at 3 a.m. Finally, they would have a last round (or first one?) in the morning at 7 a.m. Like with her previous relationship, this turned into a solid routine.

Goro, unlike her previous exes, had suggested they only have sex on weekends. "Everything in moderation," were his words, "especially fornication." Or perhaps, he'd planned to free up weekdays to screw her sister.

Anyhow, the past didn't matter now. Only numbers.

After emptying her double espresso in one gulp, Ichiko summed all the times she'd had sexual intercourse.

The result that came up was 283.

February 16th.

Ichiko was counting her steps when she heard a smack and everything became black.

When her eyes hinged open, and the blurriness cleared, the first images that filtered in were a forehead with four deeply etched wrinkles, a head with about eleven strands of hair, and a white necktie with one, two, three ... seven slanted black lines.

"She's awake!" the man yelped, the words echoing around the room—a room with adjustable beds, antiseptic smell, and artificial flowers.

Ichiko was in a hospital.

In a flash, a doctor and two nurses rushed to her bed. They gave her a thorough check-up—luckily, she only had a few bruises and scratches—while she tried to figure out what had happened to her.

Once the hospital staff left, the man bowed to Ichiko and said, "I apologize for all this." Probably seeing the perplexity in her eyes, he explained, "While you were passing through that crosswalk, I received a text message, so—"

"You didn't see the red light?" Ichiko inquired, straightening up on the bed.

"*You* didn't see it, but it was my fault too. I didn't see *you*."

Ichiko slapped her forehead. She knew this counting habit would bring her numerous problems. Or reduce her life expectancy.

Without anything else to say, the man who had both saved her and almost killed her said goodbye and gave Ichiko his phone number, promising to compensate her.

She watched him go, before her gaze gradually drifted to a moving stretcher. On it, a woman in her thirties or forties lay with an oxygen mask on her face and an IV connected to the crook of her arm, while her ICU equipment beeped every three seconds.

No doubt, Ichiko could have ended like this. And then saying her last words on her deathbed.

They probably would have focused on numbers instead of words. For instance:

How many times had she loved? 0. True, she'd had three boyfriends but she had never loved any of them. Perhaps because they had never loved her back.

How many goals and dreams had she accomplished? 0. Sure, she liked accounting—sometimes to irrational levels—but it'd never fulfilled her. It was more like a junk food career. A vocational McDonald's.

How many times had she found a place where she belonged? Once again 0.

How many times had she met people who didn't find her odd? Also 0.

How many times had she felt lucky? 0.

How many times had she felt pretty? 0.

How many times had she felt happy? 0.

Ichiko dropped on her back and bit off a sigh. Why did the most important facets of her life also have the lowest figures? She had no idea. All she knew was that numbers wouldn't give her the answer—they never had.

IT'S NOT ME, IT'S YOU

"Listen, it's not you, it's me." With a groan, Youta slammed the car door shut and stepped in front of Megumi. "Let's cut the crap. Actually, it's you."

She bared her canines, squinting her puppy eyes. "What the heck are you talking about?" She surveyed her surroundings. "And by the way, why do we have to break up in a fuckin' parking lot?"

"I wanted us to have dinner at the department store." He pointed at the concrete ceiling. "But I don't think my patience can stand another meal with you."

She snorted. "Where were you going to take me, huh? McDonald's again?"

"You know why I always take you there? Because the noise of the people covers that ugly sound you make when you eat."

She furrowed her ungroomed brows. "What sound?"

"It's like mice fucking."

"Mice fucking," Megumi repeated slowly, as though practicing the spelling of the words. "Speaking of that, I've been wanting to tell you something for a while: you suck at sex. Both the time and size are short. And shit, even a turtle would thrust faster than you."

"Oh, yeah?" He stepped forward until their lips almost met. "And you suck at sucking. Why the hell do you have to use your goddamn teeth every time?"

Megumi cupped her mouth with her hands. "It's not my fault. I have long teeth." She dropped her arms to her sides. "If it's terrible, why do you want me to do it so often?"

"To avoid regular sex. I have no idea what kind of nasty infection you've caught by sleeping around, but your natural lubricant smells like expired milk."

She pressed a finger against Youta's forehead. "One, I've never cheated on you. Even though I should have, so I could get a decent fuck once in a while."

A second finger joined the first one. "Two, do you know what's the worst smell in the world? Your damn morning breath!"

It was Youta's turn to cover his mouth. "How come you never told me?"

"Because you hardly speak to me anymore. When was the last time? Two weeks ago?"

"That's because you're immensely and depressingly boring," Youta said in an unamused tone. "I have more fun doing my taxes."

Megumi took a step back. "How am I boring?"

"Remember where you took us on our last date? A freaking water museum. To see what? Water! Oh my god, that was the most boring day of my entire fucking life. And it didn't help that you were as talkative as a mummy."

"When"—Megumi squinted her eyes until they became two minus signs—"did I become your personal entertainer?"

"Right, you're my piece-of-shit ex-girlfriend."

She gritted her teeth. "Do you know. How much. I've sacrificed for you?"

"Nope."

"Listen, you ungrateful fuckstard." She grabbed the sleeve of Youta's dress shirt. "I lost my friends, family, and pet because of you."

"Wait, why is it my fault?" He blinked his threadlike eyes at Megumi. "I never prevented you from seeing them."

She dug her index finger into Youta's chest. "I couldn't, because I had to keep an eye on this thirty-year-old child—who doesn't even have a nine-to-five job—twenty-four seven."

"What about the pet?"

"You sat on Mr. Kermit!"

"Oh, you're talking about him." Youta rubbed the back of his head, as though he were confessing a minor crime. "Anyhow, who the hell keeps a frog as a pet?"

"Me!"

"But why did you put it on a pillow?" He combed his bed hair with his hand. "Well, you had your revenge, didn't you? You threw my Mr. Nemo out of the window."

"I should have thrown _you_ out of the window."

Youta tsked. "I can imagine you doing that—considering how violent, demented, and unfeminine you are."

"What the fuck do you mean by unfeminine?"

"Half of the stuff that comes out of your mouth is fuckin' swearing—and sometimes with spit. Also, you never shave your goddamn armpit hair. At least trim it a little! I've seen bushes shorter than them. Lastly, could you wear a bit of makeup and clothes that aren't T-shirts? I'm sorry to tell you this, but you aren't a natural beauty."

Megumi kicked Youta's left knee. "One, are you living in the eighties?

Being a woman doesn't mean being girly anymore." She did the same with his right one. "And two. How dare—all right, tell me what's the problem with my appearance."

"Your eyes are so far apart I get dizzy when I look at you," he said, massaging his abused leg with one hand, "and your breasts are so small I have no idea why you bother wearing a bra."

She let out a hysterical laugh. "You can talk! You aren't a looker either."

"What's wrong with me?" Youta touched a trio of fingers to his cheek.

"Nothing," she said, "you're perfectly ordinary. Too ordinary, I'd say. I'm sure if I searched a crowd, I could find your clone."

"What are you waiting for?" He faced away from Megumi, folding his arms into a sideways eight. "Go find him."

"You know, that's exactly what I should do." She mimicked his move. "No, it's what I should've done long ago."

"Go. I wish you luck. And hope the other guy gives you a good fuck."

"You dickhead." She spun around. "And you—send my condolences to the new girl, because she's going to get bored to death in bed with you. She might even become a lesbian."

Youta faced her, a grin playing on his lips. "You're just jealous. You can't handle the idea of seeing me with someone else."

"How about you?" Megumi mirrored his facial expression. "Picture me unzipping a man's pants, getting down on my knees, and taking every hard inch of him in my mouth."

He cringed in mock pain. "Ouch for him."

"Shut up. Then picture me taking off my skirt and sitting on his hard-on. Raw. Then me twisting on top of him until he says, 'Megumi … I'm … coming.' Then me getting down from him and blowing him again as he bursts in my mouth. Finally, me swallowing and telling him, 'You taste amazing. You're the crème de la crème.'"

"Record it and show it to me," Youta uttered in a robotic tone. "I might even jack off to it. "

"I knew it! You don't give a shit." Megumi's palm shoved the left side of his chest. "You don't fuckin' love me."

"You're right, I hate you," he said. "I hate you so much it gives me an erection."

"Oh yeah?" she said. "I hate you so much it gives me diarrhea."

"You shitbag."

"You asslicker."

"You clitrubber!"

"You handfucker!"

Youta and Megumi glared at each other, panting, sweating, and heating up. By then, a group of onlookers had lined up beside them. Some exchanged muted whispers. Some took discreet photos. Others filmed with their phone's cameras, possibly to upload the recordings to YouTube.

"You ... feel better, don't you?" Youta said, shattering the wall of silence between him and Megumi. "After letting all that bad stuff out."

"Guess a little," she admitted, letting the words float around them for a while. "How 'bout you?"

"I feel"—he touched his sweaty shirt pocket—"greatly relieved."

"Good." Megumi stared at an invisible point in the distance. "And I'm sure you'll feel better tomorrow, and the day after, and so on. Now that I'm out of your life."

"That means we've officially broken up?"

"Yup, I never turned down the offer."

Youta scratched his lowered head. Lifting it with a sunrise smile, he said, "That's great—because that means I'm single. So I can date anyone." His eyes, after roaming around for a while, finally met Megumi's. "For example ... for example ... you."

She let out a cackle. "What garbage are you saying? You just dumped me."

"I don't know what I'm saying ... that's why I want to figure it out. Can I? I mean, can we?"

Megumi averted her enraged eyes. With pouty lips, she muttered, "Why do you wanna date me? I make weird mice noises when I eat."

"Mice are cute, aren't they?"

"My eyes are too wide apart."

"That's cute too. Like Hello Kitty."

"I smell like expired milk during sex."

"Okay, I exaggerated there."

"How about the hating me part?"

"It's easy to hate someone you love," Youta said, "because even the tiniest thing that person does can destroy your whole world."

"And I can destroy your world?"

"Like an asteroid."

"Okay, maybe you wanna date me for real." Megumi pointed at him as though recognizing a suspect. "But why should *I* date you, Youta?"

"Because I'll improve my pelvic skills, check out my morning breath problem with the dentist, and buy you a new frog—and try really hard not to squash it with my butt."

Megumi exhaled. "No need. I don't care that much about your performance in bed, and I'm sure my morning breath doesn't smell like roses either. As for the pet, I'd prefer a cat. It's cuter. And less likely to die under your weight."

"That means," Youta began, "you accept my invitation for dinner?"

She outstretched an arm, head tilted to one side. "Only if you try to notice good things about me this time. And no McDonald's."

He clasped her hand, as if clinging to a lifeline. "I will. Actually, I already spotted one."

Shoulder to shoulder, with the crowd still gawking at them, Youta and Megumi stepped away from the car and hopped into the elevator. They punched the button number two together and ascended to the next floor.

MY PERSONAL SUPERSTAR

"Why do I have to paparazzi a classmate?" Takeshi asked, inspecting my instant camera as if it were a rare artifact.

"Because he's not only a classmate," I said. "He's Sataro Wataya. Sa-ta-ro Wa-ta-ya."

"I know his name. But it's only that: a name."

"And you're only a paparazzi for today." I shot a glance around the crowded classroom. "I don't want anyone to overhear us. Stop talking and go."

"I think you should take the photos yourself."

"Negative," I whispered. "If Sataro Wataya finds out I'm doing that, my life's over."

Takeshi furrowed his hairy eyebrows. "Don't you think you're exaggerating a little too much? Wataya isn't an actor or a rock star. He's just a university student."

"You clearly haven't been a fan of anyone."

"Everyone's a fan of someone."

"Anyway, this isn't about you or me. It's about Sataro Wataya." I peeked at my phone. The digits on top of my wallpaper—Sataro Wataya's Twitter photo—displayed five p.m. "His class is about to finish. Get your ass moving."

"Okay, Ms. Number One Fan." Takeshi strolled out of the classroom with my camera hanging around his neck.

Fantastic. I'd finally possess exclusive, everyday photos of Sataro Wataya. Photos I could carry around in my pocket. Photos I could put in an album. Photos I could kiss again and again while rolling around on my bed.

Damn, why did time have to pass so slowly? That was the definition of infinity: to wait for the person who's bigger than the universe to you. Or for news of him.

57

After a series of eternities, Takeshi came into the classroom with my instant camera. "Done."

"You're the best!" I bowed so many times my head almost fell off. "How can I repay you?"

"I'll think of something. For now, enjoy these." Takeshi spread the photos like poker cards on my desk.

I glued my eyes to them. To a profile shot of Sataro Wataya in the hallway, showing his perfectly shaped nose. A front shot of him at the cafeteria, revealing his perfectly white teeth. And my favorite, a back shot of him in front of a urinal, exposing nothing, but my libido was satisfied nevertheless!

"You should laminate these photos," Takeshi said, slumping into his chair, "before they dissolve with your saliva."

"Great idea." I sponged them with the sleeve of my sweater. "Maybe I should frame them too?"

Takeshi heaved out a sigh. "Instead of looking at his photos, why don't you go to see the real person?"

"Are you for real?" I scolded. "He and I live in different worlds. And I don't have access to his."

"Of course you do." Takeshi rested his protruding chin on his first. "I saw Wataya getting into the Rock Club. The one at the Student Activity Center."

My ears perked up. "But what should I say if I go?"

"Simple," Takeshi chirped. "That you came to check out the club. You don't even have to join it."

"And what should I say to Sataro Wataya?"

"You don't have to talk to him."

"You're a genius!" I rose from my chair. "I'm going now."

He gave me a wrinkled squint. "First wipe the drool off your mouth."

On my way to the Rock Club, to meet Sataro Wataya, I couldn't stop feeling self-conscious about my clothes. Damn, I should've come to classes in my summer dress. Anyway, my sweater would do; although plain—with no printing or garnishing whatsoever—it outlined my sensuous attributes. My skinny jeans achieved the same effect.

I knocked at the door with the metallic plate that read, *Rock Club*. After a couple of forevers, a guy with his face hidden behind piercings opened the door.

"Excuse me," I began, "I came to check out Sataro Wataya's Club—I mean, the Rock Club."

Piercing Person stared at my body for so long, I felt naked to the bones. With a pornographic grin, he said, "Come in, sweetheart."

Even sitting in the chair nearest to the door, I couldn't remain calm in the cramped room. Because Sataro Wataya wasn't there. And because I was not only being ogled by Piercing Person, but also by Mohawk Man and Giant

Goth. What was this? The backstage of the band Hungry Hyenas?

"What's your department, darling?" asked Piercing Person from the microphone stand on my left.

"I'm not from this university," I lied. "I'm a one-day exchange student." I could've said I liked vaginas, or even better, kicked him in the balls. But I needed to be on amicable terms with him if I wanted to get close to Sataro Wataya.

"Where d'you live?" inquired Mohawk Man from the microphone stand on my right.

"Abroad. In Kyrgyzstan."

"Can I have your email?" Giant Goth ventured from the drums.

"I forgot my password and my secret question."

Piercing Person: "How about we exchange phones, babe?"

"Mine fell into a hot soup yesterday."

Mohawk Man: "Wanna go on a date with me?"

"No!"

Giant Goth: "Do you want to go to karaoke with us?"

"Enough!" I shouted. "I only came to see Sataro Wataya. Tell me where he is."

"Sataro Wataya?" the three echoed, glancing dumbly at each other. Facing me, they asked simultaneously, "Who's that?"

I crumbled in my chair. I didn't know where to find Sataro, but I knew how to punish Takeshi.

"Ah, it wasn't the Rock Club, but the Jock Club." Takeshi rubbed the red starfish I'd made on his cheek with my hand. "Sorry, I flunked English spelling in elementary school. And high school. And last semester."

I banged my hands on my desk. "You did it on purpose, didn't you?"

"Of course not, I don't hate you that much."

"You certainly don't show me your love." I sprawled in my chair, mentally and morally defeated.

"Sure I do." Takeshi hauled his iPad from inside his desk—a temporary replacement for his broken iPhone—and held it before my eyes. "Check this out."

Sure, Takeshi. I'd like to meet this fan of mine, especially because I had no idea I had any. Tell her we can meet this weekend at any place she wants.

I clamped my mouth shut so my heart wouldn't pop out of it. Once the drumming subsided, I said, "Why. Did. You. Do. That?"

Takeshi blinked his slanted eyes. "Aren't you excited?"

"Yeah, so excited I wanna jump onto a train track." I grabbed the sleeve of his dress shirt. "I'm going to mess up. Let Sataro Wataya down. What should I do, what should I do?"

"You should cool off."

"You should call off the invitation."

"Listen," Takeshi began, resting his hands on my stiff shoulders, "you should meet your idols, because only then you'll realize that they're people like you."

For the first time, I saw light in Takeshi's eyes. With a nod, I said, "Thanks for your wisdom, sensei."

"Guess the pupil's ready." Takeshi removed his comforting hands from me.

"By the way, did you think about your reward?"

He rubbed the budding stubble on his chin, his eyes rooted on mine. "I know, lend me your instant camera."

I squinted at him. "What do you want to shoot?"

"Nothing, just everyday things."

"I hope by 'everyday things' you don't mean women's underwear." I pulled out my camera from my backpack and passed it to Takeshi.

"Many thanks," Takeshi said. "And good luck with your date. Remember, be yourself—but not too much."

I stared at my reflection in the black mirror of my phone. To be myself. I could be that.

After a Googling marathon, I picked New York Bar, a luxury hotel bar in Shinjuku, those where paying the bill came with pain. But I chose it anyway because it appeared in the movie *Lost in Translation,* featuring Bill Murray and Scarlett Johansson. The setting was perfect for an evening with my personal superstar.

Next, I selected my best clothes. In other words, I bought new ones: a one-shoulder mini-dress and double-strap high heels.

Finally, I turned up at the entrance of the hotel thirty minutes early to prepare myself psychologically. To put it another way, to drown my nervousness with the small bottle of Suntory whisky I'd bought at FamilyMart. Also, to rehearse the fifth draft of the interview I'd written for Sataro Wataya.

"Do you find the interviewer attractive?" I read to myself—at least I thought I did.

"Are you in the Drama Club?" said a minty breeze.

Sataro Wataya.

I stepped back and looked up. Above me, like a starry universe, Sataro Wataya came into sight. He exhibited a perfectly uniform smile and perfectly combed hair. Also, a perfectly fitted blazer and perfectly tight jeans. Perfect perfection.

"N-n-no." I shoved the whisky into my handbag. "I'm in the Sataro Wataya Club—I-I mean, you are Sataro Wataya, right?"

"That's correct." He leaned slightly toward me, squinting his eyes into perfectly straight lines. "And you must be Ms. Number One Fan."

"H-how do you know my name? I mean, that this was me?"

"Takeshi sent me a photo of you, so I could recognize you."

"Oh, no. Did I look good in it?"

He snickered. "I've never laughed so much on the first date."

"You laughed? Oh right, you did." I giggled. But not for long. "W-wait, this isn't a d-d-date. It's an—interview."

Sataro Wataya guffawed again. "So you prepared an interview for me."

With a nod, I fumbled inside my handbag and pulled my laminated paper. "I-I-I was planning to edit it a sixth time. S-sorry for not having prepared more, but Takeshi told me about this meeting at the last minute."

Sataro Wataya gaped at me. "So you *really* prepared an interview for me."

I heaved out a sigh. Be yourself? Screw you, Takeshi.

We got into the hotel and rode the elevator to the bar. It was like a movie. Or I should say, like in *the* movie: dim except for the yellow lamps on the seats, quiet except for the live band in the middle of the room. My favorite part was the full-length window at the back. It looked like a wallpaper featuring Tokyo's glittering night scene.

I suggested we sit at the lamp-lit bar, explaining that was where Scarlett Johansson sat with Bill Murray in a film.

"So what were their first words to each other?" Sataro Wataya asked as he lowered himself into a leather chair.

I sat next to him. "'For relaxing times, make it a Suntory time.'"

"I'll have that. How about you?"

"I'll just have a beer." The Suntory whisky I'd downed outside was still trying to crawl up my throat.

A few minutes later, the bartender slid the drinks and rice crackers in front of us. Plus the dwarf pizza and the giant plate of fries we'd ordered as an afterthought. Was it time to start the interview? But what if I said something wrong? Wait, perhaps to not say anything was worse?

"So, shall we start?" Sataro Wataya said with faux formality.

"Yes, yes. Excellent idea!" I hauled out the A4-paper from my handbag and hid my scorching face behind it.

Sataro Wataya chuckled. "I meant, start eating and drinking. But it seems like you want to do the interview first."

"W-we can eat the interview. I mean, eat while we're having the interview, or have the interview while we're eating. Whichever you prefer." I gulped my beer so fast I almost drowned.

"Either option is okay for me," Sataro Wataya said.

Better read the second question, since I wasn't inebriated enough to start with the first. "D-do you have a female Homo sapiens with whom you interact in an intimate way?"

"No, I don't have a girlfriend."

Yes! "Next question, what configuration of genes or atoms should your mating partner have?"

"Let me see ..." Sataro Wataya began in a pensive voice, "I don't have a particular physical preference. As for personality, I like women who are calm, composed, and confident."

Oh my, oh my. Like me?

Keeping the interview questions in front of my face, I picked a slice of pizza and took a bite. After finishing chewing and choking, I asked, "Has any human female been swimming in your neural ocean lately?"

"Nay. I'm not interested in anyone."

Yay. Wait, should I feel unhappy because that meant Sataro Wataya didn't fancy me?

"Let's stop talking about me." With the gentleness of a floating cherry blossom petal, he pushed my A4 paper aside and greeted me with his perfectly aligned eyes. "I want to know about you."

"M-m-me?" I stuttered. "But I-I'm no one."

"If that were true, you wouldn't be sitting here with me." Sataro Wataya plucked the interview questions from my hands and pretended to read. "When and why did you become my fan?"

"I-I—" Better stop drinking beer. Stuttering and slurring simultaneously wouldn't sound very nice. "L-l-last year, I was taking photos with my instant noodles—I mean, instant camera while I was eating instant noodles on a campus bench. At some point, I spotted a tiny star in the sky, so I angled my camera for a shot. Just then, you passed in front of me and became the highlight of the photo."

Sataro Wataya offered a five-degree bow. "Apologies for that."

"It's all right." I gave him a flickering smile. "Because I found another star that night." When I got home, I couldn't stop staring at Sataro Wataya's perfect profile in the photo. Why did I get so starstruck? Perhaps because at that time, he was minuscule, sparkling, unreachable.

He laid the A4 paper flat on the table. "You know, I don't need to ask more questions. You cleared them all up with that answer." With a perfectly wide and white smile, he added, "Right. As for your first question—no, I don't think the interviewer is attractive. She is *dazzling*."

My heart backflipped. And everything turned black.

My senses, like raindrops forming a pond, gathered bit by bit. First, my hands felt the silky texture of fabric. Then my nose registered the powdery scent of cotton, and my ears perceived the scary quietness of loneliness. Finally, my eyes met the shadowy corner of a ceiling.

I was in a bedroom.

With a jolt, I sat up and glanced around as my eyes switched to night mode. Black mini-bar. Orange two-seater. White king-size bed.

No, this was a *hotel* room.

"Are you okay, Ms. Number One Fan?"

I faced the bay window. Sataro Wataya stood there, sipping a glass of whisky. Suntory?

"W-w-what happened?" I asked.

He turned on the lamp and perched on the edge of the bed. "You suddenly fainted. I would have taken you home, but I didn't know the address. The other option was to go to mine. Unfortunately, I live in the men's dormitory."

"W-w-wait," I blurted, "y-you rented a room just for me? In a luxury hotel?"

"Don't worry, it's not a deluxe suite. Besides," Sataro began in a humorous tone, "I'm a celebrity, remember? I'm wealthy."

"Thank you very much." I bowed fifty degrees. "I'll pay you back—in installments."

"No need." Sataro Wataya rose to his feet. "You've already rewarded me with this night. It was amazing. I'll always remember it."

I gawked at him. "Y-you talk like you're leaving ..."

He nodded. "It wouldn't be good if I stayed."

"I'll leave!" I hopped off the bed. Luckily, I still had my dress on. "You paid for this room, so you should stay."

"It's all right. I live nearby. Besides, I don't want to spend the night in a hotel alone."

"T-t-then let's both stay." Wait, wait, what did I just say?

Sataro Wataya eyebrows almost reached the top of his head. "Are you sure?"

"N-no, but I think it's the only solution."

His gaping mouth eased into a warm smile. "You know, I feel bad for doing this. On the other hand, I'm glad I can spend more time with you."

"Me too." But I wasn't glad. I was madly excited!

"I'm also glad that you're okay—that reminds me, carrying you on my back made me sweat a little. I think I'll take a shower."

As soon as Sataro Wataya got in the bathroom, I texted Takeshi, *I'm in a hotel with Sataro Wataya. What should I do, what should I do?*

After an infinite minute, he replied, *Dunno. Maybe play chess with him? Check stock trends?*

I'm serious. Oh, he's showering now. Sataro Wataya is naked. And I'm in the same room as him!

Bet you just came.

I'm the one in the shower now. Naked. And Sataro Wataya is in the same room as me!

You took your phone into the shower?

Oh, I'm out now. I'm sitting on one edge of the bed and Sataro Wataya on the other.

You know. Actually, you shouldn't ...
We've chatted for too long. Talk to you later!
"Shall we sleep?" Sataro Wataya said with an impersonal tone.

Without daring to twirl around, I said, "I-I'll make my bed on the two-seater."

"I can't let you do that ..."

"T-t-then let's both sleep on the bed." Wait, wait, wait, what did I just say?

"Is that all right for you?" Sataro Wataya asked. "I don't want to make you feel embarrassed."

"N-no, I won't feel aroused. I mean, excited. I mean, embarrassed."

"Can I be honest with you, Ms. Number One Fan?"

"S-s-sure." When I turned around, my jaw opened and my mouth watered.

Sataro Wataya wasn't wearing his bathrobe but his naked skin. Oh, my. I had a first-row view of his perfectly straight shoulders, perfectly sculpted biceps, perfectly molded abs. And perfectly solid pen—perfection.

He crawled onto the bed and said, "I've desired you ever since we met." His lips brushed mine with each uttered word.

"Really, really, really?" I chirped. "I mean, you're not only interested in my body, right?"

"No, also in your heart." He gently slid on top of me and, as though they were a set of curtains, pulled the lapels of my bathrobe apart, exposing my bare breasts. "I've never had this craving before. Like, I want us to squeeze together until our skin become one, our sweat becomes one, our moans become one. Until we clim—"

"Ahhh ... ahh ..."

Sataro shifted his hands to my arms. "Are you okay?"

"I just had a ... leg cramp," I said, panting. Who would have thought? Non-penetrative orgasm wasn't a myth.

"Maybe we should sleep?"

Time to be, not who I was, but who I wanted to be.

I wrapped my arms around Sataro Wataya's neck and my legs around his waist. "Yes ... sleep *together.*"

With a sunny smile and the swiftness of a magician, he produced a condom from under the pillow. He rolled it on and, without resistance of any kind, entered me. Again and again. Each time, expanding my wet interior, squeezing a steamy moan out of me.

Oh, I had Sataro Wataya inside me. We lived in the same world. The fact filled me with so much ecstasy, I came a second time, a third, and a fourth. The fifth one, I did it right in the same second as him.

"That was like in the movies," Sataro Wataya said as he sprawled on top of me like a defeated soldier.

I nodded since I didn't have the energy to move my tongue. The only movement in my body was my trembling legs and heaving lungs. I didn't mind being like this, because the planets had aligned in my favor, because a new universe had opened before me.

Because I had reached the stars.

Since I couldn't wait to share my ecstatic night with Takeshi—leaving out the climax count, of course—I darted to his department first thing the next morning. He had public relations class.

With Sataro Wataya?

Why was he sitting next to Takeshi?

I hid behind the open door and eavesdropped. Unfortunately, other students had arrived, so Sataro Wataya and Takeshi's voice were drowned in an ocean of chatter. Fortunately, my superstar left the classroom, probably to go to his.

So I barged in to interrogate Takeshi. "Why were you with Sataro Wataya?"

"I exchanged phones numbers with him, remember?" Takeshi lifted his arms to show his innocence. "We continued texting and became friends."

"Oh, that's all. Sorry, for doubting you." Into his ear, I asked, "By the way, what were you guys talking about?"

"Men talk." Takeshi leaned back in his chair.

"It isn't in a language women can't understand. C'mon, tell me."

"Maybe it's in a language women can't accept."

"All right, then I won't tell you what happened last night." I stormed out of the classroom. When the break arrived, I slipped into my hideout behind the door. When Takeshi exited the classroom—perhaps to go to the toilet—I tiptoed to his desk and fumbled inside. As I'd predicted, his iPad was there. But now I had to guess his lock screen pattern. U for Unlock? Nope. T for Takeshi? Wrong. L for Let Me In? Incorrect. S for Solution? Bingo!

I tapped the icon of his messaging application and read the silent speech bubbles.

Sataro: Ms. Number One Fan was easier than a ping-pong match without a net.

Takeshi: What you gonna do with her now?

Sataro: Maybe have a few more games, until I get tired of playing with her.

Takeshi: Let's meet tomorrow so you can tell me more.

The stars in my sky fell all at once, leaving nothing but an infinite patch of black. How? When? Why? No, I knew why.

"What are you doing here?" Takeshi asked as he stepped to his desk. "With my iPad?"

I gripped the sleeve of his dress shirt, so hard my fist turned as white as the garment. "You brainwashed Sataro Wataya, right? You became jealous of my happiness, so you told him I was a skank."

"No, I was *worried* about your happiness," he said, "I started feeling that way after getting closer to Sataro. He's nice on the surface, but his heart is dark and sucks everything it can find. Like a black hole."

"Your heart is the same." I wiped my tears. Tears warmed by rage. "I read the texts you sent to Sataro Wataya."

Takeshi fished out a folded tissue from his jeans and held it before me. "I was just playing along with Wataya. To reveal his real game. I know it wasn't the best solution, but it was the only one I had."

After some consideration and hesitation, I received the tissue. "Why didn't you tell me all this?"

"I wanted to. When you were texting me from the hotel. But then I thought about how sad you'd become after losing your superstar." Takeshi rested his warm hands on my shoulders. "Sorry, I should have been more down-to-earth.

I should have left everything as it was. I shouldn't have tried to do the 'right' thing. I shouldn't have set up the invitation. I—"

"Takeshi?"

He lowered his head until our eyes were aligned. "Yes, Ms. Number One—Ms. Sano? I'll do anything. Kick Wataya's butt, kick my own, get you another superstar."

"I don't want any of that," I mumbled, fixing my deluged eyes on my desk. "I just want to apologize. I only care about my happiness—and you also only care about mine. So there's no one left to care about yours."

"Hey, don't speak like I don't have a life," Takeshi joked. "Actually, I'm not sure about that—I only know I don't have more tissues. Wait here. I'll go get some." He put me in his chair and flew out of the door.

I slid Takeshi's iPad back inside the desk. As I did, my hand brushed other objects. My instant camera. And scattered instant photos. Oh right, Takeshi had borrowed my camera. Should I look? If he used it to take pictures of his personal superstar, I could help him as he did for me.

I spread the photographs before me like a fan. One showed a profile shot of me at my desk, staring stupidly at Sataro Wataya's photos. Another a front shot of me in Starbucks, drinking ceremoniously a lemon juice. Another a back shot of me on campus, gazing mesmerizingly at the night sky.

My heart warmed. Right, Takeshi had always been my personal sun. Perhaps because his light had become an everyday thing for me, I forgot it was there, illuminating my footpath, filling every cell in my body with energy. Keeping me fully alive.

Spotting Takeshi entering the classroom, I tucked the photos back into the desk and straightened up on the seat.

"Do you feel better?" He handed me a new pack of pocket tissues.

I nodded, showing him the shiniest smile I could manage. "Because I found my new superstar."

SUSHI STOP

I traveled three hours just to eat sushi alone. Again, I sat at the circular counter and watched the sushi parading on the conveyor belt; again, I tried to swallow down the urge to steal the knife from the chef and stab Tatsuo in the chest.

What had been his excuse this time? Oh, yes. The specimens in his fly breeding experiment. The idea had been to use alcohol to put them to sleep, then track the traits of each generation. Unfortunately, he'd poured too much, assassinating the poor insects and forcing himself to start all over. A tragedy. But not worse than mine: waking up at six in the morning, paying for a round-trip ticket, and traveling three hours for nothing!

Well, almost nothing. I had my sushi.

I picked a salmon roe and nibbled a bite. The salty savor swept me into a sea of sensations. I could hear the cries of seagulls, the mooring boats, the waves bursting on the rocks at the beach. My eyes watered as the wasabi shot up my nose and into my brain, numbing my senses with ecstasy, convincing me that I had found my ultimate destination.

Yup, another worthwhile trip.

Tatsuo sprang the news on me a month ago. We were vacationing at Zushi beach, me sprawled on my towel, him buttering sunscreen on my back. I adored his fingers on my skin; it made me feel warm and cool, vulnerable and protected. Most of all, at ease—for being close to him and knowing that even with closed eyes.

It wouldn't last long.

"Internship in Osaka University? For six months?" I flipped around, sunscreen dripping down my back. "Why didn't you tell me before?"

He waved his hands. "I just submitted the form. Didn't think I'd get accepted. My grades aren't that good, you know that, and there were thousands of applicants. But somehow I got in."

Tatsuo always did crazy deeds on a whim—the ingredient in his personality that made me fall for him and, ironically, scared me the most.

"That's great!" I forced the words out of my throat. "It'll be tiring, though. Traveling every week." From Tokyo to Osaka was a three-hour journey by bullet train.

"I'll stay at my uncle's. No need to travel, or rent."

"Then you'll come back once a month?"

"Hard to say, because of the lab work. And there's my aunt. Her back isn't well, so I promised to help her with her chores. That'd be my way to pay her for—"

Anger boiled up inside me, but I dealt with it as I always did. I pictured a glass being filled with tap water (instead of coming from a tap, though, the water appeared from mid-air). And the glass would never overflow; it would keep guzzling water endlessly. That was enough to calm me.

I sighed. "Okay, I'll come visit then."

Tatsuo bowed an apology. Honestly, I had no other choice. I couldn't stand more than two weeks without seeing my boyfriend. And listening to him on the phone and reading his text messages would feel cold, like talking to a recorded version of him.

He left for Osaka the following month, promising to make time for me. As I saw him board the bullet train, a deep anxiety invaded me. One that rooted me to the platform. However, I reminded myself that it wouldn't be so bad. That we wouldn't separate, just be far apart from each other.

I couldn't have been more wrong.

Problems started the third week of Tatsuo's internship. Since I didn't want to be late—we only met on weekends—I took the train two hours earlier. As it arrived in Osaka, I gazed at the flaring colors of the sushi restaurants and ramen noodle parlors, the blinding glitter of the shopping malls and souvenir outlets. They often made me think of a frozen sunset. Not today. The clouds made the scenery look as if it'd been showered by volcano ashes. Had Tatsuo brought an umbrella for us?

As though summoned by my thoughts, he called. I couldn't understand his words; my brain would shut down whenever it became overloaded or underpowered. Fortunately (or unfortunately), the system would restart again, ready to receive more input.

"Sorry," Tatsuo said in his whoops-I-broke-a-vase voice. "I can't make it today."

He explained that his professor had invited his lab for lunch. The request had been sudden, and if Tatsuo refused, he risked damaging his relationship with the professor.

"I know!" I chirped. "What if I go with you?"

"The professor didn't say we could bring company ..."

"How about you ask him?"

"How about we meet next weekend?" he suggested. "I think that's best."

"But I'm already here!" I shouted in my mind.

However, Tatsuo wasn't completely at fault. I'd come too early, so he probably thought I hadn't boarded the bullet train yet. Eyes shut, I pictured my pacifying glass of water.

"Hello?" Tatsuo called out. "Still there?"

A little more collected, I replied, "I'm here."

"You must be blowing a fuse now. I'm sorry."

"It's okay," I said. "I understand."

"Really?"

"Really."

"I'm glad," Tatsuo cooed. "By the way, you're still in Tokyo, right? You haven't got on the train?"

I wanted to spit everything out, but funny, I didn't. Why did we protect the people who hurt us? Was love actually masochism in a veil?

"Uh-huh." I breathed out a sigh. "I was about to board it."

"Phew. I caught you in time."

Tatsuo apologized for the third time; I held back my curses for the tenth. As we hung up, the train eased into the station. Perfect timing. Not having an umbrella forced me to sit at the entrance's facade, watching the rain fall along with my spirit. I didn't get it. How could some people stand being far from their loved ones? How did they deal with all the traveling and the steady sense of instability?

I must have been brooding for too long because my stomach began to groan. Thanks to the rush in the morning, I'd only had black coffee for breakfast. Should I eat? I didn't want to do it alone, with Tatsuo's ghost sitting across the table. But if I didn't find food, I'd become a phantom myself.

The desperation sent me wandering under the downpour, until—hungry, thirsty, and soggy—I found a shop called Sushi Stop. Outside, I was greeted by a fish graphic and framed windows. Inside, by a circular counter and a conveyor belt where sushi revolved on their fashion stage. *Sake* featured a minimalist orange cape, *Tamago* a black ribbon fastening a yellow flat cap, *Ebi* a tiger-patterned fan-tailed jacket, *Maguro* scorching pearls tucked inside a black dress.

I tried them all. In less than ten minutes.

Never in my life did I eat so fast. Was it the hunger? The anger? Either way, the sushi was incredible. Each bite sent waves of adrenaline swirling throughout my body—on the way, washing away the fury and grief that had almost eaten me, spraying in the glee and joy I had craved all along. No, my trip hadn't been a disappointment. It hadn't been tasteless after all.

Even though Tatsuo didn't show up from that day on, I waited impatiently for each weekend to come to Osaka. To stop by Sushi Stop and keep enjoying its fabulous food.

As time passed, the fresh flavor of the sushi became a stale solitude. Other customers came to the shop, but being alone among them made me feel even lonelier. That would stop soon.

"Regular customer, huh?" the chef commented.

I gave him a shaky smile. "You could say that." Why was Mr. Handsome Sushi Chef talking to me? Not that I'd been hoping for that. Okay, maybe a little. The weirdness of the situation, though, overshadowed my excitement; after all, he'd never said anything apart from the customary, "Welcome!" and "Here is your order."

Mr. HSC groaned. "Actually, I hate small talk. It's like a slow mental death."

"So, what's your 'big' talk?"

"It's not *that* big. I'm just curious, why do you come here alone every weekend? You're not that type."

"What type am I then?"

"Youthful and noticeably attractive," he said in a faux-formal accent.

I must have turned as red as the tuna sashimi on my plate because Mr. HSC chuckled.

"Relax," he told me. "It's against policy to flirt with customers. Plus, I bet you have a boyfriend."

"Because I'm *noticeably attractive?*"

Mr. HSC nodded. "And you always look like you're waiting for someone."

"I didn't notice."

"Your boyfriend must have problems with punctuality." Like a meerkat, Mr. HSC straightened up and scanned his surroundings. "He never shows up."

"What happened is ..." What to do? If I told him the truth, he'd laugh at me. Or worse, feel pity.

Squinting his slanted eyes, Mr. HSC set down his chef hat on the counter. "Look my shift's over. How 'bout we go to the izakaya around the corner? You must be fed up with raw food, and the place serves the best sake and grilled skewers in Osaka."

"What?" I sprinkled drops of matcha tea on my sundress. "But, I-I'm waiting for my boyfriend."

His lips curved into a smile. "I'm sure we have time."

A napalm of emotions burst inside me. Guilt. Fear. Excitement. Well, not every day a sushi chef invited you for dinner.

With his leather jacket and his long, pirate hair fluttering freely in the wind, Mr. Handsome Sushi Chef looked even more handsome. As we walked side by side down the sidewalk, I stole glances at him, feeling like a criminal. But what for? Eating with someone didn't count as cheating; same with hugging and dancing. Besides, it was Tatsuo's fault. He'd been the one who'd left an empty seat beside me.

My worries faded when I saw the izakaya. How great! It had paper lanterns that resembled hornet nests, seats as high as flamingos, a bar that had the size and shape of a piano. Mr. HSC and I sat in a quiet spot in the center of it. Noticing us, the chef took our orders.

"Is anybody home?" Mr. HSC waved the menu before my listless eyes.

"Sorry," I said, wishing my mouth hadn't hung open like a fish. "I haven't gone to a restaurant in a while. Except for yours."

"Your guy doesn't take you out?"

"Not very often."

"A homebody?" he ventured.

I slumped my shoulders. "I wish he was."

Soon the chef reappeared with the sake and the grilled skewers. Top quality menu, as Mr. HSC's had promised. The sake warmed my stomach and soul, the skewers melted my mouth and mind. However, since I'd eaten only sushi in Osaka—and for so long—tasting another food felt like a betrayal. *Only this one time,* I swore to myself.

My tongue loosened by the sake, I asked the usual, "Can I ask you something?"

"Sure," he said.

"Why did you invite me like that all of a sudden?"

"I have a confession to make. I've had a girlfriend for about two years."

"T-that's fine," I blurted a little too loudly. "We're just having dinner."

"And she canceled ours today."

I chewed over his statement. "So, you're using me as a substitute?"

"You're making it look too ugly. I just wanted to make use of my unexpected free time."

"I'm a filler ..."

"Not at all." Mr. HSC poured sake into our cups and offered a toast. When I didn't reciprocate the gesture, he added, "Guess my confession ruined the mood."

I shook my head. "It's just—don't you feel guilty for going out with me without telling your girlfriend?

"*Ex*-girlfriend."

"What? You broke up with her?"

"Just now." He grinned a pearly row of teeth. "I haven't told her yet. She's clueless."

"I'm confused too. Why are you dumping her?"

Mr. HSC peeped at his phone before tucking it into his jacket. "'Cause this isn't the first time she's stood me up."

"I know that feeling—but you don't want to, uh, give her a last chance?"

Mr. HSC scowled. His wrinkles—deepened by the luminosity of the lanterns above us—added a few years to his face. "I don't want to gamble my time away."

"Maybe she's been busy?"

"Sometimes people get busy just for the sake of being busy. It's their way of telling their dear ones that they love them but don't enjoy spending time with them."

His words reached my ears as knives. Perhaps Tatsuo didn't enjoy spending time with me anymore? Or worse, preferred to invest it in another girl? Finally meeting its limit, my imaginary glass of water toppled over and shattered into a trillion of shards.

"Sorry, I'm talking too much." Mr. HSC offered me a miniature bow.

"It's all right," I said. "I don't mind listening to your personal stuff."

"I didn't mean too much about me. Too much about *you*."

I dissected his revelation. "You know about my boyfriend? How?"

"We're drifting in the same boat." He beamed at me, then at the serene surface of his sake. "And I think it's time we return to land."

"Dunno," I said. "It's not that I don't want to break up with him. I just can't."

"So you come to Sushi Stop instead?"

It wasn't that I didn't know how to answer. I just couldn't.

"You know," Mr. HSC began, his eyes still locked on his drink, "now and then, walking through the desert of life, you stumble into an oasis. And you get stuck there, because it's so fresh and beautiful, because it's terrifying to return to the sand, the sun, the sweat. But remember, you can't stay in that refuge forever, surviving on only shadow and water. You need food. Shelter. So you either have to abandon the oasis or your life."

I always tried to fight back my tears. They always defeated me.

Mr. HSC leaned forward, without going over the friend line. "You okay?"

"It's just my glass of water overflowing," I muttered. "By the way, did you prepare that speech?"

"Of course," he said in a playful voice. "From the first day you came to the shop."

"You shouldn't have wasted your time."

Mr. HSC flashed his sparkling white teeth. "Something tells me I didn't."

Closing my eyes, I forgot about everything. I forgot about bullet trains, waiting lines, ticket counters, cramped toilets, sleepless nights on a seat. The feeling of exhaustion that never left my body. The feeling of anxiety upon arriving at a city that wasn't my own. And the feeling of detachment upon reaching my hometown without knowing who I was anymore. I finally understood. By trying to be near Tatsuo, I had distanced me from myself.

I knew my path now.

At some point, I stopped waiting. Just like Mr. HSC. That's why I didn't ask Tatsuo why he'd avoided me when he came back to Tokyo—nor when we finally parted ways. And I didn't feel bad about the whole episode, or resent him for it. In the end, that period of my life faded from my mind like drawings in wave-washed sand. Most of it is gone. All that's left in me are the memories of those quiet afternoons, eating at Sushi Stop.

CUDDLE CAFÉ

On his way home after work, Yukio took a detour. The destination: Akihabara's electronic marketplace—heaven of geeks, gamers, and gadget lovers. Not that he wanted a new laptop or fancied the latest PlayStation game. Nope. His target had warm flesh instead of a cold metal case. A warmth to melt this winter out of his body.

And what a freezing winter. Despite being cushioned by a sea of parkas, despite wearing a thick one himself, Yukio still shivered.

Not for long. Clinging to hope, he kept chasing the red Google Maps marker until the blue dot, his location, sat right on top of it. He gazed up. Right before him, stood a nondescript two-story building. Nothing else. Just frost and a torn ice skating poster. Had Yukio gotten the wrong address? Perhaps the shop had stopped business. Perhaps it hadn't survived Japan's merciless economic blizzard.

"Hello, sir," greeted a high-pitched voice.

Yukio looked up to face a girl dressed in a rose-patterned nightshirt and flame-colored slippers. She must have had muscles of steel to not to feel cold.

"Want to cuddle with a cutie for a couple of minutes?" She beamed a kittenish smile.

He widened his eyes. Yes! He'd finally found the place.

The Pajama Girl led him up a stairway. At the top, he reached a door with a billboard featuring a pajamaed woman, petite, curled seductively on a cozy futon. Above her, in bright yellow letters, said "Spoon Cuddle Café." So this was the "co-sleeping specialty shop" he'd stumble upon on the Internet. The other side of the door revealed a narrow corridor with rooms veiled behind curtains of rainbow-ranged colors—orange, peach, mustard—different flavors for different kinds of emptiness. Yukio would have to make a choice.

As though reading his mind, the Pajama Girl rang the reception bell. Instantly, the curtains stirred and three girls emerged from behind them, lining up in an orderly fashion before Yukio, eyes down. Probably students paying their own living expenses.

The Pajama Girl gestured toward them. "Which do you fancy?"

Yukio gulped, his throat dry. He'd never had the privilege of picking from a group of glamorous women—with tight legless animal pajamas. Left: a voluptuous panda with plump lips and pillowy breasts. Middle: a cute koala with sleepy eyes and small complexion. Right: a slender cat with long eyelashes and lustrous legs. Yukio was as nervous about selecting one as they were about being selected. But anyhow. He had to play this forced game of love at first sight.

He pointed at the koala.

The other girls retired to their chambers while the chosen one stood rooted to the spot, still staring at the floor. Why her? Not even Yukio knew. Maybe not knowing had been the reason; unspoken words filled with invisible meaning. Meaning that perhaps could only be felt by hand.

Hand. Yukio thought the Koala Girl would grab his and lead him through her red curtain. Wrong. She just ambled toward it alone, silently, making him trail behind like a shadow. No, maybe he wouldn't find coziness here.

The room was fancily decorated. A heart-shaped wall lamp bathed the room in a reddish hue. A futon held a folded blanket, a Pikachu doll, and stuffed animal pillows. On the back wall, hung a blackboard with today's specials written in chalk.

Customer sleeps in girl's arms (3 min)—1,000 yen
Girl gives customer foot massage (3 min)—1,000 yen
Girl sleeps with head on customer's lap (3 min)—2,000 yen
Customer and girl stare at each other (1 min)—1,000 yen

Yukio mentally converted the cost of the first packages to fit their adult cousins, which he—ashamed to admit it—had purchased before.

Customer sleeps with girl (3 min)—825 yen
Girl gives customer cock massage (3 min)—600 yen
Girl gives head to customer (3 min)—750 yen

The lower price shocked Yukio. Maybe a woman's warmth was worth more than her body.

"Do you need an introduction?" the Koala Girl called out coldly from behind.

He shook his head. "It's pretty self-explanatory. I'm just having a hard time deciding."

"When in doubt, follow the herd." She pointed to the uppermost item.

Seeing him nod, The Koala Girl marched to the bed. There, she clicked a timer and slumped onto it with her legs sideways, supporting her slim figure with her skinny arms. "And remember. You can't touch the *forbidden areas.* And no undressing—except for your jacket. Understood?"

"Understood." Yukio hung his parka on the hook behind the door and dropped onto the futon, shaking his head. The whole process felt like a purchase. A transaction. And the services—paying for a stare? Human neediness had definitely reached its peak. But Yukio was already here, so he might as well surrender to momentum. But not to disappointment; without warning, he felt a soft breast rub against his right arm, and a set of delicate fingers glide across his chest and grasp the left arm. The movement had been so subtle, so silent as if he'd been touched by a gentle breeze.

Yukio flipped to the side. As soon as he did, his chest pressed against the girl's chest, his knee knocked against the girl's knee, his clean-shaven chin brushed over and settled itself on her chin-length bob. Then he didn't move. He just remained motionless, inhaling her eucalyptus perfume, feeling her warmth transfer to him, enjoying the silkiness of her skin through her tight animal pajamas. Inside that cocktail of sensations, he forgot everything. He forgot the chill of the streets. He forgot the emptiness piercing his heart. He forgot that he had feelings to forget.

"My name's Atsuko, by the way," the Koala Girl said in a steamy whisper that heated his chest.

"I'm Yukio." He prayed to heavens not to have a hard-on. "Is there an extra fee for talking?"

Atsuko giggled, tickling his belly with hers. "C'mon, we're not that businesslike here. This is a place to relax after all."

Her sudden transformation surprised Yukio. Perhaps what he'd seen a few minutes ago hadn't been coldness, just inexpertness and nervousness. Even professional comforters could feel uncomfortable.

"Who are your customers?" he inquired. "If it isn't too much to ask."

"Mostly otaku and bachelors," Atsuko said. "You know, people who don't have anyone to blanket their hearts." She looked up, tickling Yukio's nose with her short brown hair. "Something tells me you're not one of them."

A chill ran down his spine. "How did you know?"

"I'm good at reading people. Or I should say, feeling them."

"Really?" Yukio blinked at her.

"Nah." Like a puppy searching for a biscuit, Atsuko buried her tiny nose in a crease in his shirt. "I can smell it in your clothes. Sakamichi Ice Perfume."

"You're good ..."

"I hug people every day, you forget?" Atsuko chirped. "Plus, I used to sell perfumes in a department store."

Yukio peered at the two teeny swellings under her koala pajamas. "So why did you decide to switch to, uh, this?"

"You make it sound like I'm a sex worker."

"No. I mean it's so ... different."

Atsuko tickled him with a giggle again. "Just kidding. Anyway, the reason is, I study at UTokyo."

Yukio blinked a few times. "So?"

"If you knew about the stress. God. With luck, I can sleep five hours a day—and I can't rest after class because I'm supporting myself."

"But why this job?"

"If you think about it, it's perfect for me. I can earn money and catch some sleep at the same time."

Yukio smiled. "You've become a nocturnal animal."

Atsuko beamed back. "Right, a koala."

"You haven't had a chance to close your eyes, though. How about I let you rest from now on?"

"You're so nice," she said with a charming cat yawn. "Well, good night."

So they did so. They shared no more words, just the silence of the room and their warmth that had already melded into one. Yukio found it amazing how people could communicate so much with only their bodies. Say, *I'm here for you,* without uttering a single word. Just as now. A now he wished he could extend into forever.

Of course he couldn't; before he knew it, Atsuko's timer went off, stinging his ears like raging hornets.

"Rise and shine." She unattached herself from Yukio and sat up.

In a gust, winter rushed back to him, freezing the core of his body and the memory of Atsuko's calidity in his mind. Dammit, the best moments in his life were also the most momentary ones.

"Want something else from the menu?" she asked.

Yukio scrubbed his disheveled hair. "Sorry, but I—"

"Was it that bad?" Atsuko whined, frowning her raven-black eyebrows.

"Don't get me wrong. I liked every second of it. It's just that I have to go back to my apartment."

"Oh right, the wife's waiting." Atsuko rose and bowed down. "Thanks for choosing Atsuko Airlines. We hope you had a comfortable flight."

With a goodbye and a promise to come back, Yukio paid at the counter and descended the dark stairway. As he did, he replayed in his head the relaxed exchange he had with Atsuko. She'd been more professional than Yukio had expected, quickly dropping the subject of his partner. Nor had she asked, *You'd rather hug a stranger than her?* Truth be told, he didn't know the answer himself. Perhaps he'd find out when he arrived home. *Arrive home.* The thought made him anxious. He was bringing bits of Atsuko with him. Her words, her warmth, her femininity.

And her scent.

As soon as he reached his apartment, Yukio took off his T-shirt and tossed it into the washing machine. Then he washed himself; or rather, brushed and scrubbed and rinsed until he almost peeled off his skin, until he no longer smelled Atsuko's flowering tree perfume. Yes, he'd done a good job.

Or overdone it.

"What's with all the soap and shampoo?" Rin asked dully to the ceiling. "You smell like a sachet bag."

Yukio flipped around on the bed to face his girlfriend. "What happened is"—*think, think, think*—"today at the store, I had to stand next to a Christmas tree. A real one. You know how they smell."

"What else did you do? Hug the tree?"

"I ... I had to carry it around."

"Complain to your boss," Rin said, addressing the roof again. "I don't wanna wait till the End of Time to shower again."

"You also take your time."

"Because I'm a *woman*."

"Right," Yukio mumbled. "As if women had more body parts to wash."

"It's the hair, dummy." Rin sifted her waist-long ponytail through her fingers. "I'd shower in fifteen minutes if I cut mine."

"Go ahead."

Rin snorted. "I thought you didn't like girls with short hair."

Yukio rubbed his bald chin. "Dunno. Maybe they don't look that bad."

"Talking about hair, did you see a brown one in the bathroom?"

Yukio froze. Since neither Rin nor he had dyed their hair, it could only belong to Atsuko. Dammit. He'd been so focused on hiding smells he'd completely forgotten about visual evidence. What now? His girl would find out he'd paid another to cuddle with him. The shock would be strong enough to shatter their four-year relationship.

"No, I didn't," Yukio said. "Why?"

"I'm tired. Gonna sleep now."

Rin said a drowsy goodnight and curled up in the blanket with her naked back to him. Yukio had seen it so often lately, he'd memorized each detail: the trench-like spinal cord, the rock-sharp shoulder blades, the hill-high buttocks. Sometimes he'd run his fingers throughout that topology. And sometimes she'd yank his hand away. And sometimes she'd wriggle closer to the wall. And sometimes she'd groan, "I told you, I'm tired. Go to sleep." Then Yukio would shut his eyes and sigh silently in the darkness.

Tonight, though, he didn't touch a hair. He'd been paralyzed by how Rin had dismissed her discovery. Perhaps she didn't care much about the hair that'd found its way into the bathroom. Still, didn't she want to know to whom it belonged?

Or maybe she already knew.

"What?" Atsuko blurted out. "Your girlfriend is sleeping with someone else?"

"Yup." Yukio looked at Atsuko's from the softness of her nude thighs. This time, he'd picked the customer's-head-on-girl's-lap package. "And I'm sure it's not just *sleeping* as we do."

"How d'you find out?"

"Easy. Your hair is light gray—I only thought it was brown because of the lighting in this room."

"Smart," Atsuko remarked. "But not very smart of your girlfriend. Why talk about the strand in the bathroom? Why not keep quiet?"

"That's her style." Yukio locked his gaze on the reddened ceiling. "Show the clues to hide being a suspect."

"How's that?"

"Like a murderer helping the detective. Since his 'intention' is to find the person who killed the victim, it cannot be him."

"But you can't close your case yet," Atsuko said. "That hair could belong to anyone. To a friend, to a dog, even to a commuter who fell asleep on her shoulder."

"Actually, I've been doubting her for a while. Rin has been ... how to say it ... *inaccessible* lately. At first only with sex, then it got to a point she even refused to cuddle."

"Maybe she hasn't been in the mood?" Atsuko suggested.

"Dunno. But she's surely in the mood for the other guy. She spends almost every weekend at his house. She doesn't call it that, of course. But 'traveling with girlfriends.'"

"Oh, that's ... bad."

"Thanks for an understatement," Yukio joked.

"So what you gonna do now?"

He breathed out a sigh. "Wish I knew."

"Poor Yukio." Atsuko stroked his forehead with her gentle fingers, a gesture that made him feel like a child in the womb. "I think you need a hug more than ever."

"Sorry. Didn't bring enough money."

"I didn't mean *that* kind of hug." Softly, she lifted Yukio from her lap and wrapped her fragile figure around him. Not like before. She offered him her whole being, her whole warmth. Touched, Yukio hugged her back, and the two stayed like that. Still. In silence. One sharing pain, the other comfort. One leaving behind loneliness, the other welcoming companionship. Opposite feelings that, mixed together, gave birth to a new one. Happiness.

"You're not feeling cold, right?" Atsuko asked Yukio.

"I will once I leave this room." He clung to Atsuko even tighter. "I wish I never had to let you go."

She pressed her heated cheek against his and, in the same way she'd done the first time they'd met, whispered into his chest, "Then don't."

Closing his eyes, Yukio let himself get lost in Atsuko's arms. The embrace of a woman, he realized, was one of man's most indispensable needs. As babies, they received it from their mothers. As teenagers, from their girlfriends. As adults, from their wives and daughters. When that resource wasn't available, they'd go hunting for it in a bar, a red-light district, or a place like this, where they could at least get a sparkle of it. To feel warm for a fleeting moment. To temporarily melt the icebergs they carried inside.

Yukio had no idea how long they'd held each other. He just remembered hearing the timer go off again and again. Remembered Atsuko falling asleep in his arms. Remembered *himself* falling asleep in her arms. Only one thing he knew for sure. He would never let her go.

GHOST IN THE WASHING MACHINE

Rump, rump, rump—the washing machine woke Junko. In a blink, she sat straight up in bed and peered at her phone through slitted eyes. She shuddered. Because it was two a.m. Because she wasn't doing the laundry.

And because she lived alone in the one-bedroom apartment.

Her heart thumping in sync with the washing machine, Junko slipped out of bed and stared at the moonlit veranda. From here, she could only see the appliance.

Was it broken? No, no matter the damage, the washing machine wouldn't turn itself on.

Which meant that someone had started it. A stranger? But why would one barge into her apartment to do laundry? To be on the safe side, she inspected the veranda's sliding door. Closed. Then the front one. Locked.

It couldn't be her boyfriend Kazuo either. He would've called and wouldn't have come in the middle of the night to use her washing machine. Same with her mother and landlady. Besides, Junko would have heard them leave the apartment.

That left only one suspect: a ghost.

What to do, what to do? When there was a fire, you called the firefighters. When there was a robbery, you called the police. When there was a haunting, who did you call?

Perhaps she should phone Kazuo? No, tomorrow he had an early meeting at Panasonic's headquarters. And what if her apartment didn't have a ghost?

Junko had to deal with this herself. She took out a knife from her plastic storage cabinet—a knife wouldn't be much help against a ghost, but it gave her courage—and pushed the veranda's door to the side. Nothing. Only the clay vases she had made in fire-red sunsets, the folding chair where she sat to watch coffee-accompanied sunrises. And an empty laundry basket.

Junko tiptoed toward the washing machine. It trembled and grumbled.

Rump, rump, rump. The analog digits displayed thirty minutes, the time she always selected.

She stood in a spinning trance until the cycle ended with its customary *ding.* So they wouldn't get musty, Junko hung the clothes on the laundry pole: her faded "Go Girl" T-shirt, her "Boss Babe" sweatshirt, the tattered jeans she wore while making pottery.

And Kazuo's white dress shirt. The one he'd infiltrated into her closet in case he had to sleep over and rush to work the next day.

Junko fished the garment out of the laundry bag and buried her nose in it. Instantly, the scent of her boyfriend's laundered shirt enveloped her. It always reminded her of cotton bed sheets, a sunbathed blanket, a sizzling iron on linen. Home.

Still a bit unsettled, she returned the knife to the storage cabinet and headed back to bed. Had everything been a dream? A nightmare? Or was a TV show playing a prank on her? Junko had no idea; she only knew that she wouldn't sleep much tonight.

"So a ghost washed your clothes last night." Kazuo peeked inside the haunted washing machine, then at the clothes fluttering on the laundry pole. "You should hire it to clean the floor and the dishes."

Junko scowled at him. "Take this seriously."

"Let's think rationally." As a supervisor of logistics, he enjoyed organizing reality into blocks that fit together perfectly. "Why would a spirit want to wash your clothes?"

"Maybe it thought they were *its* clothes. Maybe the previous tenant died and doesn't know it yet. And now they're doing the last thing they did before dying. The laundry."

"Good theory," Kazuo said, "but I have a better one. You pressed the *Delay* button by mistake. Or the washing machine did it itself 'cause it's broken."

"It put my clothes inside too?"

Kazuo stroked his white, clean-shaven chin. "Then there's only one explanation. You've begun to sleepwalk."

Junko squinted at Kazuo. "You mean I went to the veranda, put the clothes into the washing machine, started it, and returned to bed. All while sleeping?"

"That's the only logical explanation."

"No, not logical at all. I would have noticed if I'd sleepwalked."

"Not really. You would have been asleep."

Squeezing her eyes shut, Junko sighed. "So we'll never find out the truth."

"We will. Next week."

Right. Once Kazuo moved in, they'd uncover whether she had sleepwalked or not. Or rather, once he moved *himself* in. Most of his belongings were already in her apartment: his silver laptop, his white dress shirts, his black suits, and stuff not good enough to be useful or cheap enough to be thrown away.

As a result, her apartment—although bigger than Kazuo's—became an overstocked warehouse. A doomed game of Tetris.

But that was all right. Living together would tell them whether their upcoming marriage would float or sink. Solidify or dissolve.

The days passed and Junko found it harder and harder to wait for Kazuo's permanent arrival. Not because she wanted his presence in her apartment (she loved Kazuo more than the idea of living with him). She just couldn't wait to solve the enigma of her washing machine, which still woke her every night at two a.m.

What if she did it herself? By staying awake until morning? If the washing machine didn't start, it would *indeed* mean that she'd been sleepwalking like a zombie, that ghosts only lurked in horror movies.

As soon as she came back from the travel agency where she worked, Junko bought a Pike Place brewed coffee (she'd heard it was a caffeine missile) and avocado salmon rice (she'd read it was an energy grenade), and took them to the tea table. Once full, she hauled her potter's wheel out of her wardrobe and started making pottery.

She wasn't sure why the craft had drawn her. One day, while washing a bowl, as if a spirit had planted the idea into her, she thought, *I can not only clean, but also make one of these.* That same afternoon, she joined a pottery workshop in Shibuya. Since then, she had made tea cups, tea bowls, and other clayware whenever time allowed, dreaming of opening her own studio in the future.

Tonight, perhaps because it was late, pottery didn't make her dream, it made her sleepy. Energy depleted. Luckily, she had a personal battery charger.

Junko fetched her phone from her tea table and called Kazuo.

"It's almost twelve," he scolded playfully. "Not feeling sleepy yet?"

"I'm not planning to sleep." Junko shared her insomniac scheme with Kazuo, skipping the trivial details so he wouldn't fall asleep.

"Sure it's a good idea?" he blurted. "Lack of sleep can affect your memory."

"I don't remember having read about that."

"And your mood."

"There's nothing wrong with my mood!" Junko cupped her mouth. "I'm sorry. It's just that I want to get to the bottom of this mystery fast."

"Speaking of fast," Kazuo started, "There's a question that's been running around in my mind."

Junko rose to her feet. "Which is—?"

"Do you think we're rushing into marriage?"

"Why? You think we are?"

"No." He let the ghost of the word linger for a moment. "I think *you* think that."

She fiddled with her a-little-too-tight engagement ring. "But I already said yes."

"We don't always say things with meaning, or know the meaning of what we say."

"What's that supposed to mean?"

"It means what it means."

Junko glanced at the army of cardboard boxes enclosing her. "Actually, I haven't thought much about our wedding. Not because I think we're going too fast, but because everything has *happened* too fast."

He fell silent for a few seconds. Then, with a weary sigh, he said, "Yeah, I'm probably overthinking this."

Kazuo wanted to accompany her in her vigil, but Junko persuaded him to go to sleep. Otherwise, he'd go to work with only half a brain tomorrow. It was already two after all.

Wait, two a.m.

She turned to the veranda, expecting the washing machine to quiver to life under the full moon. She waited and waited. Nothing.

Junko squinted blurrily at her bed. Should she go to sleep? But what if the washing machine came to life as soon as she closed her eyes?

Refusing to lose the battle with a home appliance, Junko resumed making pottery so she could escape from boredom, and ate dark chocolate so she could benefit from their stimulating effects.

The clock struck three a.m.

Four a.m.

At five, Junko's eyelids could no longer fight gravity. How about napping for one minute? She fetched her blanket and wrapped herself in it like a cocoon, wishing she could stay here forever. It didn't matter if she never became a butterfly—wait, was that buzzing a swarm of bees?

Rump, rump, rump.

Her eyes snapped open like just-cooked clams. She hadn't been sleepwalking after all. She just hadn't been awake enough to confirm what she already knew: her washing machine was haunted.

Junko sprinted to the storage cabinet, snatched the knife, and ventured onto the dawn-bathed veranda.

She fixed her gaze on the washing machine. It seemed to rattle with more fury than usual. Was this an illusion created by her drowsy brain? Better nap for a while. She had thirty minutes.

As soon as they passed, Junko left her knife on the folding chair and yanked open the washing machine. Inside, she found the laundry she was supposed to do that weekend.

And a doll.

With frightened curiosity, Junko held the toy between two fingers and lifted it from the washing machine. It was a Licca-chan dress up doll. Without clothes. She would have been completely bare if not for her hair—copper red like Junko's—draping her nippleless breasts.

How had the Licca-chan found her way into her washing machine? Junko had no idea. All she knew was that doll didn't belong to her. In fact, she hadn't owned a one since her elementary school days.

Who owned this one?

Kazuo sat across from Junko at the tea table to eat the curry rice she had prepared—a frequent scene on weekends. And it would become even more common once they became husband and wife.

"So did you find out whether you're sleepwalking?" he asked.

"If I did sleepwalk," Junko began, "then I went out in the middle of the night to buy a Licca-chan doll and threw her in the washing machine together with my laundry." All this assuming she fell asleep in her blanket.

"A Licca-chan?"

Junko pulled the doll from one of Kazuo's empty cardboard boxes and dropped it onto the tea table.

Setting down his chopsticks, her fiancé grabbed the doll and cradled it as if she were his daughter. "Thanks for finding her."

She blinked at him a few times.

"It's your birthday gift," Kazuo said.

Right, Junko's birthday was around the corner. "But why a doll? I'm twenty-one, in case you forgot."

"When I saw she looked like you, I couldn't help myself. And you like working with your hands. I thought you'd enjoy dressing her up."

"Thank you." She pointed at the doll, still stunned by Kazuo's sudden interest in children's toys. "She lost her clothes, though."

"What I wanna know is how I lost *her*. She was supposed to be in my wardrobe."

"Then there's a ghost after all ..."

Kazuo chuckled. "There should be a rational explanation for this."

"Which one?"

"I accidentally threw her into my suitcase when I was packing my clothes. Then you accidentally threw her into your laundry basket when you were washing them."

Junko frowned. "And the washing machine ate her dress?"

"Maybe it got stuck inside, somehow."

"What about the box?"

"Guess it dissolved or something."

"You're trying so hard to be rational that you're starting to sound irrational!" She covered her mouth with both hands. Shouting at Kazuo wasn't in her romance résumé, and surely it wouldn't land her a job as a wife.

Junko put on her single-breasted coat, her mid-calf boots, and hurried to the door. Before turning the knob, she swiveled around and said, "I need some air."

Kazuo, his mouth agape, rose from the tea table. "You've never needed air before."

"Not true. I have lungs like everyone else." Saying goodbye with a wave, Junko rushed out of the apartment and stepped down the L-shaped staircase. Below, she ambled under the crimson evening sun.

But to where?

Her feet, or rather the subway, took Junko to the swarming streets of Shibuya. More specifically, the pottery workshop she attended. They didn't open on Saturdays, so she just looked in from the outside: at the clay cups aligned like runners on their marks; at the potter's wheels facing each other like people in a meeting; at the table itself, dark like the stage of a canceled show.

Was her show canceled too? Once Junko married Kazuo, she wouldn't be able to open her pottery studio. She would be too busy being a wife, a housewife, and—when the time arrived—a mother.

The buzzing of Junko's phone pulled her back from that imagined future. She dug it out from her coat's pocket. Kazuo had messaged her.

Did you get enough air? I didn't mean to upset you.

She let out a breath and texted, *I apologize too. Actually, I'm not bothered about something you said. But about something I haven't told you about.*

Want to tell me now?

Junko stared at her phone for a minute—a minute she wished she could stretch until infinity. *I think we should slow things down between us.*

But we've been together for a year already ...

I mean, between us and our marriage.

After a couple of seconds, Kazuo typed, *You definitely need more air. It's okay. I don't wanna make you feel suffocated.*

Junko bit her icy lower lip. *How about you? Do you need to think about us too?*

It's not necessary, he replied. *I'm always thinking about us. Especially about you, and how the only air I enjoy breathing is the air around you. Cream, chlorine, chocolate. Those smells remind me of home. Also the smell of clay. I can help you open your pottery workshop, because it's your dream, and I want us to build our dreams around each other.*

She chewed her lip even harder. Tender words were the ones that made her heart ache the most. Why didn't she have any for Kazuo? They might come to her once she spoke face to face with him. Once her head ceased to swirl.

Junko left the pottery workshop and took the subway back to her apartment. When she said, "I'm home," she found out Kazuo wasn't. Not in the bathroom, not on the veranda. Not anywhere.

After a minute or two, a message from him appeared on the luminescent surface of her phone.

I went back to my apartment. I think you need more space, at least for now. Sorry for leaving my boxes behind. Also, sorry for not helping you with this washing machine issue tonight. But you can call me whenever you want. I'm here for you.

Junko held her phone to her chest, finding it difficult to breathe.

She spent the next few hours resisting the urge to call Kazuo. Perhaps he was right. She needed some space.

But what should she do with it?

Anyway, there wasn't much space left with Kazuo's cardboard boxes lying around; one by one, Junko pushed and pulled them around so they wouldn't get in her way. Funny. She was clearing away the debris of the world she had destroyed. Or rather, stopped.

Should she make it spin again? If she did, she'd get trapped in its continuous revolutions. Like in the past few days. But if she left it still, she risked losing her future with Kazuo.

What was best? To go left or right, up or down? The world around Junko whirled—no, not only the world.

Rump, rump, rump.

Enough. She couldn't endure this anymore.

Sliding out a knife from the storage cabinet, Junko shoved her way into the veranda. *Stop, stop, stop!* She lifted her arm and slammed the knife down into the washing machine. The force of the strike sent her to the folding chair. Stabbing a home appliance—had she gone mad? Why not try to stab a ghost? A thought?

She had no choice but to wait.

When the washing machine finally dinged, she grabbed the garments and hung them on the laundry pole. Would she have to do this again and again? Her mind began to numb, as well as her hands, now soggy and chilly. Luckily, only one piece of clothing remained. Kazuo's immaculate white dress shirt.

Junko brought the shirt to her nose and breathed in. Cotton bed sheets, a sunbathed blanket, a sizzling iron. How could she have forgotten? She needed this smell as much as she needed food. It gave her energy, joy, and who knew, perhaps strength to face the foggy future.

"No, not foggy," she whispered to herself, pulling out her phone from her jeans and beaming at its luminous screen. "It looks clear now."

After hanging the dress shirt on the laundry pole, Junko called Kazuo. He picked up right away.

"Sorry for acting weird tonight," she said, spinning her token of marriage around her finger. It didn't feel tight anymore. "I mean, these days, especially at night."

"It's okay," he replied calmly. "But why the sudden change?"

"I found out there's too much air here. Too much space. So ... could you come back, please?"

To build their dreams around each other, huh? It didn't sound that bad.

THE TRASH THINGS PROJECT LOVE

Miyako knew that a modern disease was to stuff your apartment with possessions. She never imagined she'd suffer from the opposite.

It all started because of an argument with her boyfriend Tokiya. One concerning a toothbrush.

"Why did you buy this?" he asked, holding it as she stepped into the bathroom.

"So you can brush your teeth." Mimicking the action, she added, "Put it in your mouth, then move your hand up and down."

"You're funny. But seriously, why?"

"Why not? You sleep here six days a week." With a teasing grin, she said, "Or do you like using my toothbrush? You have that kind of fetish?"

Tokiya scratched his crew cut. "This makes me feel like I've moved in."

"You could. It's easy. Just stay over one more day a week."

"Living together before marriage kills relationships."

"But we should live together. We've already been a couple for what? Two years? Besides, it's like a test."

"You only test something when you think it has a problem."

"Or when you care about it."

"I think I'll go back to my apartment." Tokiya dropped the toothbrush back into the cup. "So I can think about this moving-in-with-you issue."

"But why do you have to do that without me?"

"You know me. I make better decisions when I'm alone."

Miyako hated when he was right because there was nothing left to say.

That night Miyako did what she always did when she was down or upset: housework. It kept her mind occupied. And without energy to feel pain or sadness.

She began with dishwashing (in the bathroom since she lived in a one-bedroom apartment without a kitchen). Once done, she arranged the tableware by size in her plastic storage drawers: the chopsticks and spoons in the first drawer, the teacups and glasses in the second, and the bowls and plates in the third.

Next, on the veranda, she gathered her clothes and folded them by color in her chest of drawers. Her red dress went together with her orange sweater, her green T-shirt with her turquoise hoodie, and her purple blazer with her violet tank top.

During a break, Miyako fished her iPhone from her sweatpants. No calls or texts from Tokiya.

She swallowed her pride and sent him a message. You don't have to move in. We're okay as we are.

While waiting for a reply, she slumped at her low table, turned on her laptop, and deleted unused files and folders. In 2019, cleaning up your computer must count as domestic work.

Seeing no response from Tokiya, she typed another text. Please come back. I'll throw away your toothbrush and let you use mine.

Miyako resumed her chores. By the time everything was tidy, she was too exhausted to check her phone, so she crawled to her futon and threw the blanket over her head.

Actually, she was too frightened to check her phone.

Tokiya never texted back. Or called. So for the following days, after her shift at IKEA, Miyako did nothing but wipe, wash, dust, dry, and brush her apartment.

When she was cleaning her bathroom, she spotted the blue toothbrush she'd bought for Tokiya and examined it like an archaeologist. What should she do with it? She could use it after her current toothbrush wore out—but using the toothbrush that'd ended her relationship would leave a bitter taste in her mouth.

And so, Miyako stepped out of the bathroom and threw the toothbrush into the plastic bag containing her non-burnable trash. Then she looked around. She'd expunged Tokiya from her apartment.

No, not quite.

She sprinted to her chest of drawers and pulled out a contour pillow (those with a little valley in the center to prevent neck pain). Tokiya had bought it to put it under her buttocks during coitus, claiming it'd helped them achieve a better angle.

Miyako tucked the pillow inside her burnable trash, feeling as though she were burying the corpse of their relationship. The next day, she disposed of the garbage and cast a look around her apartment. Done. Tokiya didn't exist in this apartment any longer. She felt lighter, like she'd shed some pounds. And it wasn't only because those items had been linked to him, but also because, even though they hadn't occupied much space in her apartment, they had done so in her mind as mental baggage.

Now she was a little freer.

A little happier.

Miyako sat cross-legged and reflected on this new finding. This new feeling.

And she took a dead-simple yet potentially life-changing decision.

The next morning, Miyako took the day off to focus on The Trash Things Project, as she'd start calling it. But which possession to throw away? Each item served a purpose in her daily life.

How about changing her lifestyle?

If she stopped cooking and only ate out, for example, she could get rid of her mini-fridge, dishes, and plastic storage drawers.

Miyako called the waste management people, and the next day they came with a pickup truck to take away the unwanted items. After thanking them and paying the fee, she cast a glance around her apartment. It looked bigger. With more space, more air. And less visual noise.

To celebrate this, Miyako went to a restaurant across from the street and treated herself to a big bowl of sashimi donburi, with golden sea urchin, peal-like salmon roe, and fatty tuna that resembled pieces of marble.

Nothing like restaurant-made food.

Dumping her plastic storage drawers made her wonder whether she could do the same with the chest of drawers. Why did she need drawers at all? Clothes didn't need darkness and dust wouldn't stick to them just because they were outside. And so, she pulled out all of her clothes and arranged them (by color) in the corner where her fridge used to be. It looked weird, like a colorful stack of papers. But it was all right because they didn't get in the way. And she wiped her floor every day, so hygiene wasn't an issue.

Looking at her clothes, a realization hit her: since it was summer, she could get rid of her winter coat and denim jacket (she could buy new ones next year). Also, she didn't need her orange pajamas. Why not sleep in underwear? Come to think of it, why had pajamas even been invented? She wouldn't need her dress either since she'd bought it to go on romantic dates with Tokiya. Same with her lingerie.

Miyako folded all those garments into her backpack and wandered the streets until she spotted a homeless person in a park. He had more beard than face, and more grit than clothes, but looked friendly.

"I don't need these clothes anymore," she said, fishing them from her backpack and holding them in front of him. "Would you like to have them?"

The man took them, pressed them against his nose, and inhaled deeply. With a lewd grin, he said, "Sure."

When Miyako was dealing with her chest of drawers, she found her books in the bottom one. So the following morning, she resolved to get rid of them.

But should she keep some? She flopped down on the floor and lifted the first book. Everyday English Expressions. Since high school, she'd always fantasized about living in America or Canada, in a big house with a garden, free from Japan's workaholic culture. But she never put any effort into learning English. Could she even order at McDonald's? Anyway, Japan wasn't so bad. After all, it was one of the countries with the highest safety index, life expectancy, and economic influence. Besides, you could learn pretty much anything on YouTube.

The second book was a driver's handbook, which Miyako had bought to get a driver's license. But why should she get one? Tokyo Metro could take her anywhere while reducing her risk of a car accident and enabling her to do things while she commuted. In any case, she wouldn't go to many places now that Tokiya was gone.

The third book was the novel Bleak House. She'd purchased it to improve her English reading skills and become knowledgeable in English classics. She couldn't finish it; she'd put it down every time she finished a sentence. It felt like a chore. (Entertainment shouldn't feel like that, especially since life was short!) She had more fun doing real chores.

The rest of the books belonged to Tokiya. He'd had the bad habit of bringing books to her apartment and leaving them here. She sighed. Exes were like emotional mosquitoes.

Miyako dumped her books inside her backpack, Googled the second-hand book shop nearest to her apartment, and went there on foot. She got only a few coins for the books. But she didn't care because, for the first time, she was the author of her own life.

While eating breakfast, under her low table, she found a text she'd forgotten to throw away. Guide by Guitar Gurus. Holding that book, she made another discovery: she had a possession she'd never used.

Her Yamaha acoustic guitar.

She walked to the corner wall and picked it up by its neck. Its body was gleaming vanilla. The sound hole and tear-shaped pickguard made the guitar look like a crying cyclops. Tokiya had promised to teach her how to play the guitar. In the end, the only thing he ever taught her to play was the skin flute. Should she use the guide to learn solo? Nah. Now that he was no longer part of the band Miyako and Tokiya, she didn't feel like learning.

She Googled the nearest second-hand instrument store, and went there to sell her still brand-new guitar. It didn't make her feel depressed, but when she returned to her apartment, she felt in the mood to listen to sad songs.

The Yamaha Guitar reminded Miyako of her photos with Tokiya.

She pulled out the first photo album from the cardboard box. In it, they were holding hands in front of a Christmas tree as tall and shiny as a lighthouse. Cuddling on his couch like a cat couple. Singing karaoke in a room shaped like a small concert hall. Being showered by cherry blossom petals so white they resembled snow. Watching fireworks exploding with the intensity of Big Bangs. Freezing moments of happiness.

Miyako cried, wishing her tears were acid so they would dissolve the photos.

To alleviate the pain, she tossed the photo album back into the box and pulled out another one. This one featured her friend Aya—or rather ex-friend. She'd met her in college, but their friendship dwindled after they graduated. Which was strange. Back then, they used to do everything together. Cook together. Cry together. Get heartbroken together. Get over a heartbreak together. Feel lonely together. If there was such a thing as soulmates, they were twin souls.

Perhaps Miyako was the problem? Maybe she made people feel stuck? Maybe she was human quicksand?

If she threw away these photos, she'd never see them again. Unlike the other possessions she'd discarded, these neither had a price nor could they be bought back. What should she do or not do?

It was okay. Those memories were stored in her mind. True, some would fade with time, but that was okay; that would mean they weren't precious enough, and therefore not worth keeping.

She threw the photo album back into the box and sealed it with tape. How to get rid of photos? Right, her mother was an avid photo collector (especially when it came to Miyako's photos). So the next morning, Miyako went to the post office and sent the cardboard box to her parent's house in Toyama.

"What's going on?" her mother asked in the phone call that night. "You're moving out of your apartment?"

"No," Miyako replied, "I'm moving on."

Only three items remained in Miyako's apartment: a low table, a laptop, and a futon. The most essential of items—wait, she didn't need her low table. Since the furniture was already so close to the floor, why not use the floor instead? If she used her futon as a floor pillow, she could get rid of the latter. True, the floor pillow was thicker and harder, but she could lay back on the futon whenever she tired of sitting. She was a genius!

Now she only possessed—this time for real—the most fundamental items: a laptop and a futon. No, that wasn't quite right. If she went to libraries or Internet cafés, she wouldn't need a computer. How about her phone? Screw it. Since she didn't have a boyfriend, friends, or a job that required you to be available 24/7, she wouldn't need it anymore. To call her parents, she could use a public phone or Skype in a café.

Miyako had forgotten about the things in her bathroom … if she used her hands to wash her face and let her body dry by itself after showering, she wouldn't need towels. She could use shampoo as soap. As for her toothbrush and toothpaste, she wouldn't need them if she cleaned her teeth with toothpicks or by gargling water with salt.

A realization struck Miyako: she could get rid of her futon if she used her clothes as a pillow, blanket, and mattress. Sure, the floor would be hard, but she'd eventually get used to it.

Miyako had a revelation: since she'd gotten fired from IKEA (for not going to work), didn't have a boyfriend, and didn't go to any social events, she could get rid of her makeup. And the rest of her clothes—except for her T-shirt and jeans, which she could wash and dry every day since it was summer.

And so, she disposed of her makeup. As for her extra clothes, she tucked them in her backpack, went to the homeless man she'd visited last time, and they repeated last time's scene (including the sniffing part). After that, Miyako ate omelet rice in a cheap restaurant and returned to her apartment. Sitting cross-legged, she cast a glance around and gave a teary smile to herself.

She was free. She was happy.

She had nothing now.

MY LAST EIGHT HUNDRED EGGS

"The good news is that you don't have ovarian cancer," the ob-gyn said, his oval eyes locked on the pad containing my blood test results. "The bad news is that you have a low ovarian reserve."

So my insufficient appetite, hyperactive bowel movements, and uneven period weren't a death sentence. I would have jumped of happiness if it wasn't for the doctor's last statement.

"Simply put," he continued, "you have approximately 800 eggs left."

I straightened up on the hospital bed. "*800 eggs?*" Was I at the Shinjuku Ladies Clinic or the supermarket?

"Let me explain," the ob-gyn began. "A woman is born with a fixed number of 2,000,000 eggs, and she loses them as she ages. Only 400,000 remain when she enters puberty."

"How about when she's twenty like me?"

"200,000 or more."

My eyebrows furrowed. "How come my count is so low?"

"You have a rare condition called *ovarian underproduction syndrome*. In other words, your ovaries created fewer eggs than they were supposed to."

I slumped back on the bed to digest this sour news. No, it wasn't that upsetting. "This disorder isn't life-threatening, right?"

"Not to you, but perhaps to your future child if you're planning on having one. In the sense that he or she might never be born."

"But 800 eggs are still a lot, aren't they?"

"They are—except a woman loses about 34 eggs per day."

I consulted my mental library. "I thought only one or two eggs were released each month."

"Correct. But the rest die every day, like the other cells in the body."

I used the immaculate ceiling as a whiteboard to make the calculations. "That means, I'll lose all my eggs in about three weeks."

The ob-gyn nodded. "Therefore, you should consider fertility treatments. Like oocyte cryopreservation, which consists of freezing your eggs to be used when you need them."

"What's the cost?" I asked.

He gave me an exorbitant number.

"I don't have that money," I blurted. "I'm just a university student."

"How about adoption?"

"I would find raising a stranger's child weird."

"Then I suggest you start *family planning* as soon as possible."

The advice was sensible—except I didn't have a husband or a boyfriend.

766 eggs left.

I skipped my classes today. Instead, I went to a restaurant in Shinjuku and ordered a omelet rice. According to my unscientific theory, if I ate eggs I would produce more or strengthen the ones I already had.

Of course, I couldn't solve my problem only with food. I needed a plan. *Family planning* as the ob-gyn had put it.

And it was a *real* problem. One of my dreams was to have a daughter, so I could style her hair and buy her lovely dresses. And of course, hear her say her first "Mama," teach her a second sentence, and change her last diaper.

All right. I had to stop dreaming and focus on my ovarian nightmare.

To become a mother, I would have to quit university—not that I'd mind since I hated animal science (I'd mistakenly chosen the department after having enjoyed a book about chicken. Turned out, I didn't like poultry, but the poetry in the writing). Sure, my parents would beat me to a pulp—or I should say, scrambled eggs—but this was about my life. And my future child's.

And my future partner's, which couldn't be any random guy or sperm donor. I had to find someone who valued fidelity and responsibility. And quickly.

732 eggs left.

I bought a yellow dress (to make sure I caught men's eyes) and went to an overcrowded underground bar in Shinjuku (so no one I knew would see me).

But which man to choose? My humble requirements were: round eyes, round cheeks, and round chin—in short, a baby face. I had no idea why, but a science magazine stated that we were attracted to people who looked like us.

After one hour and two whisky sours with egg white, I spotted a twenty-something who fit that description. He sat four stools away from me, gulping sullenly from a foamy beer. When he glanced in my direction, I shot him a come-here-stupid smile. But he didn't. Just brought back his eyes to his beer and kept looking gloomy.

Screw indirect signals.

With a newly ordered whisky sour with egg white, I squeezed through the shoal of people, perched on the stool next to the guy, and presented myself. Chika. Warily, he did the same. Eguchi.

Pleasantries over, I dropped my carefully crafted line. "Would you be kind enough to answer a few questions?"

Eguchi narrowed his eyes into half circles. "Is this a survey?"

"I'm gathering data to find a suitable partner." I pulled out my phone from my purse and opened my note-taking application. "Question one: do you like girls?"

"Yup."

"Right answer. Question two: do you have a girlfriend?"

"Nope."

"Am I your type of girl?"

"Absolutely."

"Awesome." I scrolled to the bottom of my phone's screen. "Last and most important question: at what age do you want to have kids?"

"Kids?" he blurted, as if we were talking about elves. "Let me see—maybe at thirty."

"Wrong answer." I hopped off the stool. "Goodbye."

"Wait, wait," Eguchi called, flailing his arms at me. "I mean, any time's okay, as long as I love the girl."

"All right. I'll let you take a make-up exam." I leaped back onto the stool. "Personal question: Why the long face?"

Eguchi looked down. "My girlfriend and I broke up a month ago."

"Improper question: why?"

"To sum up, she got pregnant, had a miscarriage, and blamed me for having *defective* sperms."

"That must've been ... hard on you." I sipped my drink and asked, "It's not true that you have defective ... you know—?"

He shook his head. "I had a test a few days ago. My sperms are normal."

"Excellent!"

Eguchi lifted his face. "Excuse me?"

I cupped my mouth with my hands. "I mean, I'm glad you're healthy."

He nodded, staring at me as though I were a turtle with two heads. "Speaking of reproduction—why the question about having children?"

I hadn't prepared this part.

Since we had to get into a long-term relationship in a short time, I told him about my rare condition and my universal wish.

"Sounds a bit nuts." Eguchi signaled the bartender for another beer. "But glad to know you selected me."

"Not yet," I said. "You gotta pass the final test first."

He leaned a few inches away from me. "Something tells me this is gonna be insane."

"That depends—if you dare to go to the women's toilet with me." I pretended to fold origami with the cuff of his dress shirt.

Eguchi gaped at me. "You kidding?"

"I don't have time for jokes. I only have 732 eggs left, remember?"

"Okay, you convinced me." He sprang from his stool. "Let's go."

"You go first." I glanced at the neon-lit crowd. "Unless you want people to see us going inside together."

"Smart!" Suddenly not looking sad anymore, he sauntered to the girl's toilet and, shooting me a wink, vanished behind the door.

Five seconds later, I vanished from the bar.

Why? Because I only had three weeks. I couldn't waste them with a man willing to make love at first sight. Those never lasted long.

For the whole weekend, I applied the same test in other bars in Shinjuku. 50% of the participants accepted going to the toilet, 30% suggested we go to the toilet of their apartments, 20% suggested we go to the toilet of a love hotel. God. It seemed that the men of the night were better at mating than matchmaking.

Better hunt prey during the day.

630 eggs left.

I used any sources and excuses to meet men. University, public libraries, private parties. While doing so, I discovered that my "Find a Darling Before Your Eggs Die" game resembled gambling.

I bet—

102 eggs to Jojima, a biology major I met at Tokyo University. He had plenty of positive attributes: intelligence, diligence, and self-reliance. But in the end, he confessed he didn't want to spread his genes at the moment.

136 eggs to Quincy, a thirty-year-old American who taught in a private school. He was an exotic, enthusiastic, and optimistic man. Unfortunately, he had to visit his home country for three weeks.

170 eggs to Kawamura, a wedding photographer with a receding hairline. He exuded maturity, reliability, flexibility all the time. To my luck, he was married and planned to turn me into his mistress.

By the time I came out from this dating pachinko parlor, I only had 222 eggs left.

I was about to go bankrupt.

188 eggs left.

My gonadal clock was ticking. More than ever, I needed to find a man who was committed but not to another woman. Who would move my heart but not his country of residence. Who liked children but didn't behave like one.

Children. That was the keyword that would lead me to him.

120 eggs left.

Matsuyama Park had the air of a retirement home rather than a playground. It had a moldy bench, a dusty slide, and two rusty swings. Not even the natural elements lit up the place: grayish ground and balding ginkgo trees.

Plus, there were no kids.

I climbed up the slide and surveyed my surroundings. Did I get the time wrong? According to its website, the orphanage nearby brought the children here every Friday at five p.m.

Just when my hope was dwindling away, I heard tiny steps behind me. I spun around. At the bottom of the slide stood a girl of four or five. She had silky straight hair that reached her waist—not a difficult feat since she was shorter than a mailbox (I thought of a mailbox because she wore a red dress).

"You're adorable!" I let myself fall down the slide and knelt before the little angel. "Want Big Sister to tie a fishtail braid for you? I'll make you look even cuter."

"You're not Big Sister," she corrected in her Minnie Mouse voice. "You're a *stranger.*"

"You're ... right," I said. "And it's dangerous to talk to strangers. But that's true mainly with men."

"Not true. Papa is a man, and he is not a stranger."

Hold on a second. "Your father is here?"

With a miniature nod, she pointed behind me.

I followed her finger, standing up. At the top of the slide sat a man in his thirties. He had a baby face—round eyes, round chin, and round cheeks. However, his soft qualities made him look more elegant than juvenile. Or perhaps this aura was cast by his clothes: blue denim jeans, green turtleneck sweater, black blazer.

When he slid down the slide, I told him my name. He disclosed his: Hasemi.

"I apologize on behalf of Toshiko." He bowed forty-five degrees. "She doesn't get along well with strangers."

At a loss for anything witty to say, I said, "How about you? Do you get along with them?"

"Depends on the stranger." He beamed at me.

Should I consider this man a potential mate? (If he didn't have a wife, of course.) He seemed good-hearted and good-looking. True, he had a daughter—but what a lovely one!

"Don't get close to Papa." Toshiko squeezed between Hasemi and me, her palm up like a police officer.

"Toshiko." Hasemi rested a hand on his daughter's shoulders. "Go play on the swing for a while, okay?"

Pouting her slim lips, Toshiko stomped to the swing and sat on it. The act awakened a motherly pity in me.

"Apologies," Hasemi said. "She inherited her father's temperament."

I tilted my head. "But you look like a calm guy."

"Truth is, I'm not Toshiko's father. She just calls me that because I've been visiting her since she was a baby."

I leaped to my feet. "You volunteer in the orphanage around here?"

"You were looking for it?" In a playful pitch, he added, "To become a volunteer? Or to adopt a kid?"

To have a kid with a volunteer, I'd have confessed if those words didn't sound crazy.

Instead, I asked, "How about you invite me to dinner?"

"You're a daring darling, aren't you?" Hasemi said, *daring darling* in English.

"I like dares but not games."

He offered a nod. "I don't like to rush things, but time is precious. So why not?"

My heart warmed. Few people took their time to appreciate yours.

"But first tell me," he began. "Why are you in such a rush to date me?"

I lowered my eyes. Should I tell Hasemi about my undersupply of eggs? No, since I had only a few days left of fertility, I had to make myself as desirable and valuable as possible.

"Can I tell you after we know each other better?" I requested. "This is a sensitive issue. One that has to do with a deep part of me."

"No problem, I have all the time in the world." Hasemi lifted his index finger. "Right, we have to schedule our date. How about this Saturday? Same time, same place."

"Deal," I chirped.

"Where would you like me to take you?"

"To the izakaya over there." I pointed to the wooden establishment decorated with unlit paper lanterns.

He rubbed the back of his head. "Seems like you planned everything."

"I don't have time to improvise."

"I'll follow your script then." His eyes switched to the set of swings. "Okay, I should attend the spoiled little princess. See you soon."

I waved goodbye to Hasemi as he darted toward Toshiko.

When I left the park and plunged into the subway, it hit me: I'd have to wait three days to meet him.

And we had forgotten to exchange contact details.

86 eggs left.

I went—or to be more precise, ran like a mad woman—to the orphanage where Hasemi volunteered. There, Toshiko told me he would come on Monday, and that she didn't know his phone or address, which didn't sound logical. Was she old enough to lie?

52 eggs left.

Fearing the home for children would send me to one for the crazy—they'd began questioning my sanity due to my insistence on contacting Hasemi—I stopped going there. Instead, I spent the day browsing all the *Hasemi's* on social media. I'd surely find him since that surname only existed in Japan. Wrong. People from Afghanistan and Bangladesh also had it.

I sighed. *Egg*cellent

18 eggs left.

I had my head buried like an ostrich in my drawer, choosing from my few date-worthy clothes. This was my last chance. If I didn't make Hasemi love me and make love to me in the next twenty-four hours, my dream daughter would remain just that. A dream.

After defeating indecisiveness, I took my red summer dress (because men subconsciously liked women in red), my black lace thong (because only a madman wouldn't like it), and the Saint-Amour wine I'd bought a while ago (because it was a good moment to be mentally anesthetized).

When I arrived at the park, I found Hasemi sitting at the entrance of the park's slide, wearing skintight chinos, a tucked-in shirt, and a well-fitted blazer. Seeing him taking our random date seriously made my heart pump blood at double speed.

"You okay?" Hasemi asked. "You smell of grapes, and your cheeks are like tomatoes."

"Oh." I held my heated face. "I kept some grapes for a long time in my fridge, and they fermented. Who would've thought? You can get tipsy with fruits!"

To my relief, Hasemi laughed at my tasteless joke. "This will sound like a cliché, but you're different from most women I've met."

I managed a weak smile. "More *different* than you think."

Our groaning stomachs told us to go to the izakaya. Inside, we sat at the corner of the bar—the only available seat in this packed place—where I ordered smelt roe, flying fish roe, and salmon roe sushi from the chef.

"Whoa," Hasemi said, receiving his sake set. "Are you planning to build an aquarium in your stomach?"

"Not at all."

"A fish farm?"

"Sorry, I'm not in the mood for this type of jokes." I shut my eyes to avoid seeing how I'd ruined the mood between us.

Right, who was I fooling? I'd never form a family in only one night. Building a relationship took months, planning a marriage years. And finding your soulmate sometimes a lifetime.

"Apologies." Hasemi faced me and bowed forty-five degrees. "No more fish jokes, I promise."

I sighed. "Sorry, the problem isn't you. I'm just having a bad week."

"Well, today isn't a bad day." Hasemi grinned, showing a row of egg-white teeth. "At least not for me."

My lips curled up against my will. "How come you're not dating anyone? You seem to be good with women. And children."

"I'm on a date right now." Hasemi poured a cup of sake for me and him. With such grace, he could be a host in a club. "By the way, you seem to be good with children too."

I blinked at him. "Where did you see that?"

"When you were with Toshiko. You're one of the few people who's managed to stand her for more than five minutes—without wanting to slap her."

I chuckled. "She's a real a case, isn't she?"

"A really complicated one."

"Do you mind telling me about her?"

He stared at his sake like someone developing photos in a darkroom. "Long story short, Toshiko was born from an adult mother who still wanted to be a teenager. She gave birth to Toshiko in the public toilet of a park—and tried to flush her down. As if Toshiko were feces."

I flinched, unable to continue eating my roe sushi. Bizarre. While I was killing myself to give life to a baby, others were killing babies so they could enjoy their lives.

"Did the father find out about this?" I asked. "You said you knew him."

"That's right. But I ended our friendship—when he told me he wished his girlfriend had succeeded in *disposing of* Toshiko." Hasemi rocked his sake as if to erase the images he saw on its surface. "You know, people think it's a blessing to bring babies into the world. But maybe we're inviting them to hell."

"It's not true," I said, "you gave Toshiko a little heaven."

Hasemi shot me a sad smile. "Not sure if I've given her enough, though."

"She'll decide that after she grows into a healthy, happy woman."

"That's my dream." He gazed at the red paper lantern orbiting above us. "What's yours?"

My hopes with Hasemi returned after he'd shared his story—somehow, he convinced me that we could write one together. So I resolved to reveal my plan.

But I needed to test him first. "Can we talk about this in a more private place? Like my apartment?"

Hasemi's huge eyes enlarged even more. "You're *really* a daring darling, aren't you?"

"It's not courage. It's impatience."

"What's making you impatient? Your *sensitive* matter?"

"Be patient. I'll tell you about it when I'm ready."

He scratched the back of his head. "Okay, I have all the time in the world."

Still 18 eggs left.

I sat side by side with Hasemi on my single bed, our eyes locked on our feet like two inexperienced teenagers.

"So what's the test?" he asked.

I didn't fail him on it because he'd accepted to come to my apartment. Why? I enjoyed my time with him. And most importantly, I didn't have more time.

"It'll start now." Without giving regret a chance to act, I shoved Hasemi into the middle of the bed and plopped down on his lap. "Ready?"

His Adam's apple bobbed up and down. "I don't have a choice, do I?"

"Excellent. Question one: do you like girls?"

When his hard-on poked my buttocks, he said, "Does that count as an answer?"

"As evidence," I replied. "Question two: do you have a girlfriend?"

"If I had one, I wouldn't be here."

"Correct answer. Am I your type of girl?"

"If you weren't, I wouldn't be here."

"Last and most important question—would you like to love me?"

With a mellow smile, Hasemi cupped my cheeks and parted my lips with the tip of his tongue. With his forehead pressed against mine, he said, "There. More evidence that I'm interested in you."

I beamed at him. "My turn to show interest." I dimmed the ceiling lights, unbuckled his leather belt, and let it fall on the bed. His chinos, shirt, and blazer joined it. And my red dress.

"Sure this isn't too fast?" Hasemi asked.

"You said time is precious. It's even more precious to me." I pulled off my strapless bra and lace thong, followed by his boxers. With sweaty hands, I grabbed his erection firmly and slid it inside me, squeezing out a gasp from him.

"Did it hurt?" I inquired.

He shook his head. "How about you?"

"No pain." Our little foreplay had readied me enough.

"That's good, but *no* condom isn't." He fished a shiny, silver square from his jeans and left it next to his arm.

I smirked at him. "You were sure you'd take me to bed, huh?"

"No, but I had to take precautions. You know, in case I was lucky enough."

I lifted Hasemi—without detaching our lower halves—and cradled him in my arms like a baby. My tenderness, however, faded when I remembered the use of contraceptives.

Panic rushing through me, I pushed Hasemi on his back and my hips against him. "We don't need condoms. I'm safe today." Actually, it was my least safe day. A strange way to refer it, since that fact could save dream.

"How about other *dangers*?" Hasemi asked with a moan.

"I've been STI-free all my life."

"We have the perfect conditions."

Gripping his body and starting moving, whispered into his ear, "So you can come inside me. Would you like that?"

"I ..."

"Would you like to fill me up?"

"I ... I ..."

"Until my womb becomes bloated?"

"I ... I'm coming."

With my head pressed against his chest, I thrust and thrust and thrust. No one could stop this. Hasemi and I would bring a child into this world. Would she suffer as Toshiko did? No, I would protect her at all cost. Pull her out of any toilet, any sewer, any swamp. I would—

Before I could finish the thought, Hasemi grunted and pulsated inside me. I released a long sigh. Finally. I achieved my ultimate goal.

I was wrong.

When I sat to his side, I spotted pearls of sperm sprinkled on Hasemi's abs and hands.

"It can't be," I uttered.

"I'm surprised too," he said, still short of breath. "Dunno where I got the strength to hold it for a few more seconds."

"I mean, why did you do it?"

"I know you're safe today. But you never know. Besides, we just met, so we should follow a zero risk policy."

"No, no." I shook my head. "I wasn't safe."

Scowling, he wiped his six-pack with a tissue and tossed it into the trash can. "You wanted to trick me?"

"I ..." I started but trailed off.

"Into getting you pregnant?"

"I ... you said you would like to love me. We'd have had nine months for that."

"You are *different* indeed." With a somber silence, Hasemi put on his boxers, chinos, shirt, and blazer. "But not in a good way."

"I know I did something bad. And that you're mad at me."

"Honestly, I'm too shocked to be angry."

"I'm sorry. Let me explain."

Hasemi waved his palm. "No need. It was my fault too. I shouldn't have accepted to have sex with you without protection—but don't worry, it won't happen again. See you soon." With a weak wave of the hand, he exited the front door and locked it behind him.

I sat on the edge of my bed, squinting at Hasemi's dried seed in the trash can. What had I been thinking? I almost made someone a father without his consent.

Lying back, I glanced at the wall clock. Midnight. My last 18 eggs would die anytime. Together with my dream.

But it wasn't so bad, because a new one had been born.

0 eggs left.

Matsuyama Park looked livelier than I remembered. The blue, yellow, and red of the slide and swings sparkled. The ginkgo trees exhibited a gleaming green. Had I been wearing invisible sunglasses the other day?

The only detail bleaching these colors was Hasemi and Toshiko's absence. Where were they? My phone displayed twenty past five. They should have been here by now.

Or maybe they abstained from coming today? Like silently saying, *Stay away from us?* That must be it. They had abandoned me.

Slipping my phone back into my jean's pocket, I buried my face in my knees to hide my tears from no one. Why did all my dreams run away from me? Was I frightening? Embarrassing?

"Are you crying?" asked a familiar voice.

I peered down. At the exit of the slide stood Toshiko. I could recognize her jet-black hair and mini-red dress despite my blurred eyes.

"I played too long with the slide," I said. "Now I'm sweating through my eyes."

"You are lying. Chika is a crybaby."

"How come you know my name?" I didn't remember having mentioned it to her.

"Papa told me a lot about you. You like to eat fish eggs and behave crazy like a snake."

Hasemi had been talking to Toshiko about me. Did that mean I still had a chance with him?

"Where is Papa?" I asked.

Before she could answer, he showed up at her side, dressed in the same jeans, turtleneck sweater, and blazer he wore the first time we met.

"Hasemi!" I rose to my feet.

He held Toshiko's hand. "Let's go. You've played enough." They ambled away, their backs becoming tinier and tinier.

"I'm really sorry," I yelled.

"I told you, it was my fault too," Hasemi said, without a single glance around. "So no need for apologies. Or discussion."

"At least let me share my sensitive issue with you."

He halted with Toshiko to look over his shoulder. "I've been thinking about that one."

I told Hasemi about my strange disease and common dream, as I should have done from the beginning.

"Your situation sounds insane," he said. "But I can understand why it made you go cuckoo."

I lowered my eyes to my yellow dress. "Guess desperation messed up my senses."

"And your senses almost messed up my life."

"I know. Would you forgive me? I promise to never trick you into getting me pregnant again—not that you could if you wanted to."

"You're a determined darling, aren't you?" Hasemi said, *determined darling* in English.

I raised my head, my cheeks heated up. "That's because I would like to love you."

Hasemi scanned me with his owl-like eyes for what could've been an eternity. When that infinity ended, he faced to the front and carried on with his path. "You have two options: find somebody else."

I should have guessed earlier. It was too late.

"Or accept my punishment."

My heart jumped like a frog. "What is it? Sitting in the *seiza* position for 10 hours? Being whipped 1000 times with a bamboo stick? Paying a fine of 100,000 yen? I'll do anything."

"None of the above." Hasemi rested his hand on Toshiko's ball-shaped head. "You have to make a fishtail braid for Toshiko. As you proposed to her last time."

I gawked at Hasemi's beaming face, dumbstruck. No, I had no reason to be startled. He was a forgiving god, one that would rule my private heaven. Well, Toshiko's and mine.

She dashed over to the slide. "You will tie my hair. Right, right?"

I blinked at her. "You'll let me touch you? You don't see me as a stranger anymore?"

"You are not a stranger. You are Big Sister." She flashed me a row of pearly teeth.

With fake sweat returning to my eyes and a genuine smile, I told Toshiko to sit on the slide and rode down, making her giggle when I crushed behind her. Once our laughter subsided, I grabbed her silky hair and began weaving locks. Together with my dream.

ONE-SIDED MARRIAGE

My husband, Yasushi, hasn't spoken to me in a whole year. Not a nod or even a grunt. All I get are silent stares, stiff postures, and a clamped mouth.

I tried everything to squeeze words out of him.

Like begging.

"Please." I hugged Yasushi's leather shoe. "Just say one word—just one. About today's baseball match. About your paperwork in the office. Anything."

Failing that, I tried seduction.

"How about you take the day off tomorrow?" I stroked Yasushi's boxers on the bed, wearing my fishnet stockings. "So I can 'work' on you the whole night?" I giggled.

When none of that yielded any results, I relied on threats.

"Look, if you don't say something, I'll go to my parents' house and stay there forever."

From the kitchen table, Yasushi stared at me with his large glassy eyes and a frozen thick-lipped frown.

"And I'll take your PlayStation 4 with me!"

More watching and scowling.

"And those dirty magazines I found under the sofa."

Nothing.

I threw a pillow at him and stormed out of the living room. I had a short temper, but I hated fights. I preferred discussions. However, I couldn't fix a communication problem with no communication.

So, I decided to seek professional help. A quick Internet search led me to Tokyo Counselling Services, a team specialized in helping marriages thrive through reconciliation or separation. Honestly, couple therapy had never made sense to me. Why keep riding on a boat just to patch its holes?

But sometimes you love a boat so much, you stay in it even while knowing it could sink. So much, you'd do everything you can to keep it afloat, sailing through the oceans.

"Your husband hasn't spoken to you for a year?" Dr. Takahashi blurted, gawking at me with her oval eyes.

"Or been intimate with me."

"I see." Dr. Takahashi squinted as if I were too bright to look at. "But Mrs. Mizushima ..."

"Yes?" I said.

"I don't want to be rude, but marriage counseling only works when the two parties are present."

"Well ..." I glanced at the vacant space next to me on the couch. "If I could talk my husband into coming here, I wouldn't need the therapy."

"But I don't think—"

"I don't need you to think," I yelled. "I need you to help me!"

"May I recommend a group class to deal with your anger?"

"I don't need stupid anger management!"

"Remember, Mrs. Mizushima," Dr. Takahashi said, dropping her pen onto her glistening notepad. "We only shout when our arguments aren't loud enough."

I sighed. "Sorry, I'll be quieter."

Dr. Takahashi examined my face, finally picking up her pen. "Okay, let's start from the beginning."

An awkward silence followed. I hated silence.

"So ..." She jotted down words again. "Why do you think your husband stopped talking to you?"

"I've been asking myself that question for the last 365 days."

"Any theories?"

"I can't think of any," I confessed. "I didn't get on his nerves or cheat on him. Plus, the sex was terrific."

"Sometimes satisfaction is one-sided ..."

"You mean, I wasn't actually good in bed?"

"I mean, maybe you're the only one who thinks the relationship's fine."

I fiddled with my wedding ring, reviewing the shortcomings of my marriage. "We like to sleep together, but not *literally* sleep together. No matter what we do, we always wake up tangled up with each other's limbs. Sore."

Dr. Takahashi laughed. "So cute. I don't think it bothers your husband."

"Another problem is, I always misplace Yasushi's things when I'm cleaning. Like his clothes, his watch—one time I even misplaced his glasses. I have a very bad memory."

"Does he mind?"

I shook my head. "He finds it entertaining. Pretends it's a treasure hunt."

Dr. Takahashi held her thumb to her triangular chin. "Your marriage seems perfect—I think we need to think about it some more."

"If spoken words don't work," Dr. Takahashi told me in one of our sessions. "Why not try written ones?"

And so, while Yasushi wasn't at home, I composed a letter. Initially, I thought of text messaging him, but I wanted to be more personal.

Dear Yasushi,

Have you noticed that you haven't talked or made love to me in a year? I miss it. I miss hearing your husky voice, feeling your plump lips against mine, caressing your chiseled abs (okay, I haven't seen them since you stopped jogging, but I suspect they're still there, under that beer belly of yours).

I also miss how you used to wake me up by whispering into my ear, cook your awful spaghetti for me, make me feel heard, appreciated, understood.

In other words—or rather the same—I miss you. I miss my friend, my lover, my husband. So could you bring him back home?

Please?

After unintentionally signing the letter with a couple of tears, I stuck it on the refrigerator with a magnet.

It stayed there for a day.

Then a week.

When a month had passed, I grabbed the letter and set it on fire over the toilet. Once converted into black ashes, I flushed it down. Together with my hopes.

"Come on, Mrs. Mizushima," Dr. Takahashi patted my back while I lay face down on the couch. A bit of friendship had settled between us. "You can't throw in the towel yet."

"Why not?" I said, still breathing leather. "You know the saying, 'Winners know when to quit.'"

"You won't earn anything by quitting your marriage."

"My sanity?"

"You're not insane, just crazy for your husband."

With a sigh, I pushed myself up and sat straight, face-to-face with my counselor. "Sometimes I feel like I don't have a husband."

"You do," Dr. Takahashi said. "Just think about the happy moments with him."

I gazed at the ceiling fan, letting it stir my thoughts. "Yasushi used to tell me about his day. Every day."

"Unusual from a husband ..."

I nodded. "And they were all about little things—how he picked his polka dot tie instead of the striped one. What mobile games he played on his way to work. Why he felt like calling me on his lunch break."

"You didn't feel bored?"

109

I shook my head. "I love him, so nothing he says is boring."

Dr. Takahashi flashed me a warm smile. "You seem to love him a lot."

I gave her another nod. "I love him, hate him, admire him, despise him. He's every feeling I've had for the past ten years."

"And I'm sure he'll make you feel much more." Dr. Takahashi slumped into her lounge chair. "I say this because you two are in a dream marriage. And dream marriages always have a happy ending."

For the first time that day, my lips curled upwards instead of downwards. True, this wasn't a fictional story. But reality had its own magic.

As a last resort, Dr. Takahashi suggested I try the atomic bomb of marriage reconciliation tactics. Going on a date. Which is a strange thing to do with someone you see every day, someone you share your bed with. It's like trying to catch a fish you already ate.

However, I liked the idea. Yasushi and I hadn't been on a date since he stopped talking to me. I texted him that same day.

We haven't spoken in a while, but I had fun with you last time we talked. How about we hang out again? We can do it at that Italian restaurant where we first met. I'll be waiting there at 6 p.m at the same table. No pressure. But if you don't show up, I'll slice your little friend into spaghetti strands tonight.

And I pressed send.

The restaurant looked the same as ten years ago, a life-size picture. Old-style lanterns, rusty brick walls, arched glass-less windows overlooking Tokyo DisneySea. It brought my mind to the past. To the first time I met Yasushi. The only memory I could play in my mind like a movie.

That day, ten years ago, I came to this expensive place to prove that I wasn't ashamed of being single on Valentine's Day. That I could have fun alone—actually, this yearly ritual made me feel even more lonely. Anyhow, you got to show the world you're strong.

However, I displayed my bravery to the wrong people, a couple two tables from mine enjoying a double espresso. They stole mocking glances at me, probably thinking, *Look at her. She's a future old, crazy cat lady.*

I didn't mind. Let them enjoy their last happy moments together—before they began fighting about things that they wouldn't even remember. Before they were so fed up with each other they'd do extra time at work.

Ignoring them had been useless.

As I turned my eyes to my tuna spaghetti, a shadow hovered my plate. I looked up to face the guy from the couple's table. Crew cut, large lips, glistening glasses.

Great. Adult bullying as a Valentine's Day gift.

"It wasn't enough to laugh from your table?" I said, casting my eyes down again.

"I wasn't laughing," the guy said. "My date was."

"Well, go back to her. I'm busy here working on my spaghetti."

"I can't. She's not at our table anymore."

"What?" I peeked over his broad shoulder. He was right. The table only hosted two lonely espresso cups. "Oh, I get it. You had a fight with your date, she left, and now I'm going to be your backup plan. Very smart Mr. Romeo, but I don't like being the second choice." I gobbled down a mouthful of spaghetti.

"All right." The guy spun around. "I'll leave you alone then."

Before he could arrive at his table, I asked, "So what happened? What was the fight about?"

He looked back. "I didn't like the way she was laughing at you."

I swallowed again. This time my words.

That was how I met Yasushi: him losing a companion and me finding one. I was grateful. Thanks to him, I had my first two-person date on Valentine's Day. My first time not feeling lonely.

We spoke a lot. Well, it was mostly Yasushi doing the talking. I enjoyed listening to him, though.

"You have this talent for making everything sound interesting," I commented. "It's like magic."

"The magic isn't coming from me, but this space between us." He traced an invisible line from my chest to his. "A line that I'd like to shorten."

He accomplished that in less than three weeks. However, ten years later, that line became wider than ever.

Or maybe not?

With tear-blurred eyes, I spotted a shadow on my empty plate. At last.

"Yasushi!" I yelled, raising my head to—Dr. Takahashi?

"May I join you, Mrs. Mizushima?" She set herself across from me with a somber expression.

Wiping the evidence of my sobbing with a handkerchief, I asked, "Why are you here?" I'd only told her about my dating plan. Not invited her.

"Sorry for coming. I don't usually meet clients outside of sessions. But I didn't want you to spend the evening alone."

I blinked at her. "What? You knew Yasushi wouldn't come?"

Dr. Takahashi nodded. "I found it very strange that your husband wouldn't come to our sessions. So I've been doing some research, and found out he—"

"Yasushi is alive!" I shouted, cupping my ears with my hands. "He's just not speaking to me."

"Mrs. Mizushima ... I know how hurt you are, and how much you want that pain to go away. But if you don't accept reality, you'll never fix your, um, marriage."

"You lied to me." I brought the handkerchief to my eyes again. "You said it would have a happy ending."

"Because I didn't know the beginning—or rather, the end."

I knew the end.

It began with a phone call from the police. It continued with them explaining the details of the car crash, and with me explaining how I had misplaced Yasushi's glasses. It ended with me crying next to his sheet-covered body in the hospital.

From then on, he couldn't talk to me, nor could I listen to him anymore.

And it's the same now. But who knows, perhaps—if heaven or even hell exists—I'll meet Yasushi again. So he can tell me about his day.

DREAMING ROOM

When I told Yoshiyuki I wanted to carry on with our plan to go to IKEA, he thought I'd lost a screw.

"This isn't a good idea," he said as we stepped past the sliding glass door.

"It's not an idea," I replied. "It's a wish."

Our shopping began in the Living Room section, more specifically with the sofas. After a few minutes, I spotted a two-seater and, smoothing my skirt, slumped down. Smooth. Spongy.

Yoshiyuki joined me on the sofa. "What now?"

"Let's pretend we're watching a movie." I twined myself around his arm.

He exhaled. "All right."

"Which one are we watching?"

"Which one you wanna watch?"

I pondered this, admiring the rose painting on the wall ahead. "How 'bout a romantic one?"

"Dunno, I prefer action."

"C'mon, you love to watch romance too."

"Only if no one is watching me." Yoshiyuki followed my line of vision with his dreamy, disk-shaped eyes. "Maybe we should watch this movie in your apartment?"

His participation in my game warmed my heart. I wriggled closer to him. "I don't care where I'm watching a movie, as long as I'm watching it with you."

We focused on a painting featuring an old couple. I recognized it. *Forever Always,* by Octavio Ocampo. At first sight, you saw the man and the woman staring lovingly at each other. After looking closely, you'd notice that their faces could be seen as people. Perhaps the younger versions of themselves.

"Amazing," I said, transforming my awe into words. "This old couple is still romantic toward each other."

Yoshiyuki pointed at the painting. "That doesn't happen in real life."

"Really?"

He nodded. "Romance needs a lot of energy. Buying cute gifts, writing love letters, planning expensive dinners—most people get tired of it."

"What comes after isn't bad," I said. "Comfortable companionship. You know, staying at home, settling into a routine together."

"Or double disappointment, ending in a breakup."

I shifted my eyes to Yoshiyuki. "That's not how our movie ends, right?"

He smiled at me—a smile that had acted, countless times, as my second sun in the mornings. "*You* tell me. You're the director now."

Tightening my grip on his muscular arm, I shifted focus to *our* romance. And my lust. I'd become so turned on, I had an urge to turn the TV off and make love to Yoshiyuki on that sofa, thrilled by the possibility of being seen or falling off.

I associated sofas not only with sex and romance but also with the *companionship* I'd mentioned to Yoshiyuki. In short, quiet evenings snuggled with a partner, sharing that comfortable silence characteristic of couples who no longer need to impress each other.

"So, wanna buy this sofa?" Yoshiyuki's question snapped me out of my romantic musings.

With a nod, I pulled out my phone from my purse and took a photo of the tag so we could find the flattened version of the furniture in the Self-serve area.

"First item selected." I dropped my phone back into my purse. "Now to the next section!"

Yoshiyuki rubbed the back of his head. "Didn't know you liked buying furniture so much."

"I'm not excited because of the furniture." I grabbed his hand, which seemed to become smaller as the days went by. Surely my imagination. "Let's go."

The Dining section had tables of all shapes: round, rectangular, freeform—Yoshiyuki and I sat at a D-shaped one across from each other.

"What would you like to eat, honey?" I joked.

"What?" Yoshiyuki blurted, playing along. "You haven't cooked yet?"

"Of course I did. But I didn't know what food you'd like, so I prepared many dishes."

"That must have taken a while."

"I don't mind spending time on something I love. Or someone I love." I spread my arms over my invisible cuisine. "The food's getting cold. What would you like? Salmon teriyaki, pork *shirataki,* or your favorite, curry rice?"

"Curry, of course," Yoshiyuki said. "How about you?"

I rested my elbows on the table and my chin on my hand. "I'll just look."

"You sure?"

"I've always wanted to watch you eat my cooking."

"That sounds like you—not very sound."

"Stop talking and eat!"

Yoshiyuki placed his thin hands on the table. "Actually, I'm not hungry."

"Then tell me about your day," I said.

"Let's see, I sold a condo in Shibuya, bought a tie, and now I'm telling you about my day. Your turn."

"I finished my latest interior design, started a diet, and now I'm here, pretending we're living together."

"You really like the idea, huh?"

"Everyone wants a dream home with their real love."

"As long as it's the right person." Yoshiyuki glanced around like a parent who'd lost his child. "So, which direction do we go now? Left?"

After taking a snapshot of the table's tag, we dove into the Bedroom section. It reminded me of a cloud-filled sky. White. Puffy. The perfect place to sleep. And dream.

"Look at that!" I hurried toward a king-size bed and flopped down on it. Waving at Yoshiyuki, I said, "Come in, the water is nice."

He sank beside me, breathing out as though he'd come up from the sea. "I don't think this will fit in the new bedroom."

"Don't worry, it'll be a big one."

"All right." Yoshiyuki blinked his eyes shut. "Let's dream for a while."

I closed my eyes too. Not to dream but to daydream—about sleeping in this giant bed with Yoshiyuki. Despite the ample space, we would do it around each other's arms, so tight as to almost blend our bodies. Sharing our warmth. Stroking our backs. Smelling our scents. Or instead of sleeping, we'd make love under the blanket. After coming at the same time, we'd flop dead on the damp sheets, exchanging panting and perspiration. Until falling asleep.

The next morning, we would be greeted by each other's radiating smiles. And kiss, without minding our bad breath like in the movies.

"Time to wake up," Yoshiyuki said, stirring me from my lucid dream. "And keep moving."

The next section was Children's Furniture. I didn't expect it. Just like I hadn't expected my pregnancy test to show two pink lines three years ago. Unfortunately, the little one wasn't strong enough to cling to the wall of my womb. That or my womb wasn't strong enough to hold the little one.

As I ambled among the playground of green and pink, I toyed with the idea of having had the child. Would the boy/girl inherit my single-lid eyes or Yoshiyuki's owl-like ones? My rosy skin or Yoshiyuki's deep tan?

How would he/she have looked dozing in that milk-white crib?

Giggling in that chocolate-brown rocking moose?

Kicking in that mustard-yellow junior chair?

"I know what you're thinking." Yoshiyuki wrapped his arm around my waist. "Don't think."

"It's okay. It was just a collection of cells. Not a baby." I wiped the ghosts of old tears. With a weak smirk, I added, "But it would've been amazing, don't you think? To have this half-you, half-me around. Sucking my breast. Sitting on your lap. Sleeping between us."

Yoshiyuki tucked me under his chin. "Sometimes two is enough to make a couple."

"I know. Let me dream."

"This dream will give you nightmares."

I nodded, my smile gaining strength. "Let's get something to eat, okay?"

Since I loved IKEA's healthy and hearty food, I always had problems picking from the menu. Salmon fillet, Swedish meatballs, soup of the month. This time, I opted for blueberry and goat cheese salad, and Yoshiyuki for beef rib and chicken. We carried them to seats with a window view of Tokyo's night-time skyline.

"Phew! Who would have thought?" I put my fork on the table and my hands on my skirt. "Buying furniture is more tiring than moving."

"Both are tiring," Yoshiyuki said. "That's why people want a home, so they can take a rest."

"Speaking of home, what's your dream one? We've been playing my version of the Tea Party, but not yours."

He chewed on his chicken and my question. "To be honest, I don't care about the size, the furniture, or even the location of the house. As long as it's a place I want to come back to every day."

I picked at a skittish blueberry. "Maybe I can make one for you?"

"We agreed on this. From today, you have to build your own house."

I lay down my fork to reach for Yoshiyuki's hand. It was as cold as my salad. "But I don't wanna built one without you in it."

"Please ... you said coming here would help you get closure."

"I changed my mind." I tightened my grip on him. "I don't want my wish to come true. I want my *dream* to come true."

"You have to wake up."

"I want to do it next to you."

"It's not possible anymore, you know that." With his free hand, he squeezed my shoulder. "We had a dream relationship, but it wouldn't have survived in the real world, because a couple has to be committed and complementary. Romance—and sometimes love—isn't enough."

I let go of Yoshiyuki, without another word, to avoid his usual barrage of quotes.

Just because you love someone doesn't mean you should be with them.

There's a feeling that has never helped anyone: hate.
Real life has more sad endings than movies, but also more beginnings.

My strategy worked. Yoshiyuki said, "Sorry, I'm tired. I'll go home to sleep." He stepped next to me with the face of a boy who'd killed a kitten. "Want me to walk you to the subway station?"

I shook my head. "I'll have a hot coffee. I suddenly feel cold."

He nodded, his eyes hunting for an imaginary coin on the floor. "Well ... goodbye. And sorry I couldn't give a happy ending to our relationship. I wish you the best." With a wave of the hand, the last one I'd probably see, he made his way through the packed tables, until he became one with the sea of strangers.

Instead of buying coffee, I entered the elevator and exited on the Self-serve area. Usually, I'd navigate through the shelves, matching their numbers with the ones on my phone, which would lead me to the furnishings I fell in love with.

This time, I just strolled through the shelves, sightseeing. Why had I come here then?

When I reached the checkout counter, confusion swallowed confidence. What should I do? Or say? Or feel?

"Excuse me," the boy with the yellow polo shirt said before I could react. "May I help you?"

I stared at his long face and body, short of words. No, there wasn't anything I could say or do. My dream had ended, and if I fell asleep again, no one would wake me up. I was alone in this now.

"I just browsed around." I glided past the gaping cashier, head down. I didn't feel nervous, embarrassed, or any emotions at all. My heart had become an empty room. No furniture, no people, no dreams.

I'd better focus on the outside world, especially on the front door waiting for me ahead. What would I find on the other side? Reality, probably.

INK BLACK EYE

Sumire showed up to work with a black eye. I spotted it when I went to her desk to deliver a memory card containing the models she had to *embellish*. In other words, to digitally remove wrinkles, pimples, and other natural enemies of beauty.

Being a photographer, it wasn't my duty to give Sumire these photos personally, but she didn't know her coworkers yet. Nor did they know her. Not a surprise: she was self-conscious and low-key, soft-spoken and plain-featured. You could easily lose her in a crowd.

"Thanks." Sumire tilted her head. Her chin-length hair slid off her face to reveal a bruise the color of eggplant with a slight smear of mustard.

"Does it hurt?" I indicated the swelling with my hand. It matched her purple blouse.

"Only when I blink," she replied.

"How did it happen?"

"I tried to take a photo from a high angle, but my phone fell from my selfie stick and hit me in the eye. Silly, huh?" She stifled a giggle.

Regretting my intrusion, I lowered my head. "Sorry, I should mind my own business."

"Minding people's business sometimes means caring." She flashed a row of pearly teeth.

I smiled back. Great, I'd solved the enigma of Sumire's black eye.

That was what I thought.

"Again?" I blurted two weeks later, when I handed Sumire another memory card.

She looked away from the nose she was resizing and pointed to the ink splotch under her right eye. "Another selfie. From a slightly different angle." A chuckle slipped through her skinny lips. "I should leave photography to

MY (ALMOST) LIFE AS A HIKIKOMORI

professionals like you."

"Sure it was a selfie?" I asked. "Not a *couple's* photo?"

She blinked a few times. "You mean, 'couple' as in 'lovers'?"

"Please forget it." My perception had been distorted by paranoia after all. Or perhaps not.

"Still taking selfies?" I asked Sumire after another two weeks.

She averted her eyes from the freckles she was erasing and rubbed her purple cheek powder. "I told my niece to give me a kiss—she did it with her head."

This dreadful episode repeated again.

Sumire extended her hand to her red eyeshadow. "Never stare at an apple from its bottom—especially if it's on a tree."

And again.

"Remind me to never stand behind a horse again." She caressed the brown cattle brand on her left arm.

And again.

"Or a pony." The brand had moved to her left leg.

I stitched together a pattern: Sumire had an accident every two weeks. Why exactly two weeks? I didn't know what to think. Only that I had to act.

"Uh, Sumire." I ignored her lower lip, puffy like a sausage. "Have you tried the *yakiniku* restaurant across the street? It has the best grilled lambs in the neighborhood. I wonder if—"

"Sure, let's go," she said.

She must have been starving.

We visited the restaurant after work. I suggested sitting at the back—if Sumire had a jealous boyfriend, *my* eye would end up the same color as her blouse this time.

With the barbecue stove between us, we ordered pork belly, beef liver, and lamb slices—a tongue-melting and stomach-warming selection. We extinguished that blaze with frosty beers.

But it wasn't time to chill; I had to save someone from a fire.

"Seems like you'd been on a hunger strike." I pointed to the ashy mountain of meat on Sumire's plate.

She covered her mouth with her hands. "Excuse me. I haven't eaten in a *yakiniku* restaurant in a while."

"Because there's no one to accompany you?"

"I don't have many friends."

"How about a *boy*friend?"

With her chopsticks, she lifted a piece of sizzling liver. She winced when it touched her swollen lips. "A boyfriend? I—"

Rattled by a sound or shake that only Sumire seemed to have detected, she picked up her phone. She gave me a timid bow and left the table, but without heading outside or to another room. I caught snippets of her conversation. "I'm with a co-worker ... yes, we can still meet ... goodbye."

"Sorry, a friend," Sumire explained when she returned.

"Time to retreat?" I asked.

She lowered her head. "Sorry, I forgot I had to meet him—I mean, her."

I escorted Sumire silently to the subway. All the way down the escalator, she waved me goodbye, flinching every time her inflamed lip curled up. I didn't smile. A stubborn thought bothered me.

The person who called Sumire—was she really a girlfriend?

Hoping to uncover the truth, I darted down the escalator and plunged into the tide of people. On the subway platform, I joined the line next to Sumire's. She had her phone glued to her ear. Should I step nearer? No, what would I say if she caught sight of me? *I forgot I had to take the train too. Same line and direction? What a coincidence!*

Instead, I tried to read Sumire's lips. This turned out to be unnecessary.

"I told you, he's a coworker," she whispered and glanced in my direction for a few fleeting seconds. Luckily, as if I'd been made of transparent glass, she turned away. "And please don't shout at me."

On the train, I stood four people away from Sumire, then got off with her four stations later. Back above ground, I followed her across a park sprinkled with cherry blossom trees. I hid behind one of them when she stopped forging ahead to clamber up an L-shaped staircase, which led to the deck of a two-story building. The floor had five doors. Sumire entered the middle one.

I stayed behind the cherry blossom tree until the sky turned from blue to maroon, and maroon to purple. No one came in or out.

Which meant Sumire wasn't meeting a friend. But a boyfriend, who must already be in the apartment.

I sprinted in that direction, only to stop midway.

Sumire didn't need my help.

The next day, since two weeks hadn't passed yet, Sumire arrived to work neither with a new bruise nor with a bulkier lip. Still, I wanted to make sure she didn't have psychological injuries.

"I'm fine." Sumire flicked her eyes from her monitor to me. "Why do you ask?"

I gulped dry air. "Well ... you left fast yesterday."

"Sorry. I had to meet the friend I told you about."

"Sure it was a friend?"

Sumire shifted her eyes from me to her desk. "To be honest, I haven't been a good *friend* to you. The truth is—no, never mind."

"Listen," I began. "I have no idea what problems you have. I just know I wanna help you."

"Thank you. But I don't need help."

"There's nothing more dangerous than not knowing you need help."

"I'm not in danger." To punctuate her words, she gave me a nod.

I sighed internally. How could I help Sumire if she rejected my help? Perhaps by helping anyway.

Instead of going to work on Wednesday, the day before Sumire's next injury, I called in sick with the flu and took the train to her apartment.

I hid behind the same cherry blossom tree as last time—with a six-pack of dark beer. I needed to kill my nervousness. And kill time, since I'd come early to catch Sumire's boyfriend before he reached the ambush location. I'd tap him on the shoulder and tell him that if he raised his hand against her again, I would—get on my knees and beg him to stop doing it.

A decent plan, except six hours and six beers went away, and Mr. Boyfriend hadn't shown up yet. Only random people. A housewife, a schoolgirl, a salaryman. Like billiard balls, they rolled into their designated holes, leaving Sumire's untouched.

Just when I was considering buying another six-pack, my phone vibrated. When I pulled it out of my pocket, I trembled. It was Sumire.

Perhaps she knew I was surveilling her apartment? My heart drumming, I tapped open her message.

I heard you're sick. Feeling better?

I let out a *phew* that ended with a smile. So Sumire didn't suspect anything; even better, she worried about me. The thought warmed my heart.

Much better, I texted back. *Thanks for caring.*

I don't deserve your gratitude.

I gawked at the luminous screen of my phone. *Why?*

Hey, wanna eat at the yakiniku *today?* Sumire typed, ignoring my question.

I could meet her and interrogate her about her boyfriend—except she could keep him hidden in the dark. And worse, she might not let me follow her home and put the breaks on his cyclical abuse.

Sorry, I need to do something today, I typed.

Go to the doctor? she asked.

Help someone with injuries.

Oh, what happened?

I'll let you know when everything is over. Or rather, as soon as everything started.

After saying goodbye to each other, I tucked my phone into my pocket and continued surveilling the apartment.

Finally. There.

A man in his late twenties walked across the park. Crew cut, leather jacket, jeans so tight his crotch should be begging for mercy. Because of his drunken daze, it took him almost a minute to drag himself up the L-shaped staircase, where he leaned on the door in the middle.

Too late to stop him.

Fortunately, or miraculously, he lurched to his left and tumbled into his apartment—which was at the end of the deck.

To add to my relief, an hour later, Sumire ambled up the staircase and pushed her way into her apartment. She was wearing her purple blouse—and carrying a plastic bag. Takeout for her? Or for someone else?

A disturbing theory struck me: her boyfriend, jobless, and after having drowned himself in alcohol last night, had stayed in Sumire's apartment (or his) the whole day.

I made my way out of the park and up to the door of Sumire's apartment. Should I call the police? That was the smartest move, but also the slowest one. What else could I do? Knock? Kick down the door? No, throwing coal on the fire would make Sumire's escape more difficult.

With no other plan, I glued my ear to the surface of the door and listened. Inside was as silent as a morgue. Just when I thought there might be a corpse inside, a sharp sound pierced my ears. A wail.

I banged on the door, yelling, "Stop!" I did that until my fist became inflamed. Until my sweat turned my tee into a second coat of skin. Until the door swung open.

My fist stopped right in front of Sumire's forehead. I dropped it to my side rapidly. Horrified. She already had a wound. A red ring. On her left eye.

I barged into Sumire's apartment, apologizing for intruding and setting my shoes inside the door. You gotta have manners even in critical situations.

The room consisted of a single neatly made bed, a corner desk with a laptop, a curtained window from which a beam of crimson slanted in.

That was everything in the room.

Sumire stepped toward me, slowly, as if she were afraid to break the floor. She accidentally kicked a panda yo-yo. The toy had been lying next to a plastic bag with a toy package inside.

My gaze alternated between the innocent yo-yo, Sumire's injured eye, and her boyfriendless room—my mind clouded with a thick, sticky murkiness. At last, with a deep sigh, I drove that obscurity away. What came to light was equally terrifying.

"Why did you do it?" I asked.

"Can you please pretend you didn't see anything?" she said in a faint voice.

"I don't think I can do that."

Sumire erupted into tears, her hands screening her good and bad eyes. "Because no one ever notices me. Or cares about me." She sniffed back snot. "It makes me feel so lonely, like I don't exist at all. I know, I was being selfish. Pathetic. But I couldn't keep the pain in my chest anymore. I had to let it out."

I wanted to pat Sumire on the shoulder. I didn't dare. She looked like a clay statue that would crumble with the subtlest touch.

"I understand," I said. "But don't you think what you did was a bit ...

desperate?"

"I *was* desperate," she whimpered.

"Which drove you to hurt yourself ..."

Sumire nodded, her face still resting in her palms.

"But why every two weeks?"

"It was short enough to catch someone's eye and long enough to let the old bruises heal. But I think doing that made my scheme look fake."

"Now that you mention it, it was a bit systematic."

Sumire gave another shameful nod. "So, to make everything more credible, I tricked you into thinking I had a boyfriend, one that I wanted to pose as a friend."

"That means that you don't have a boyfriend."

"Or a friend."

"You don't have either?"

Sumire shook her head slowly. "I dunno why. Maybe because of my dark personality, I can't light up anyone's heart."

"That's not true."

"You're right—it must be because I lie. Like I lied to you."

I dropped my head. "I lied to you too. No. Worse. I spied on you."

"You were just worried about me."

My head rose. "You knew what I was up to from the start?"

"I saw you in the subway."

"That's why you're not surprised to see me here," I said, my conclusion confirmed by Sumire's silence. "I finally understand everything."

"I'm glad. There's just one more thing." Sumire uncovered her eyes, now both red. "Thank you. For paying attention. For caring for me. And sorry— for manipulating you. It was too disgusting. I deserve to be slapped."

As though preparing herself for the firing squad, she closed her eyes, revealing a thin cut on her eyelid. Reaching over the desk, I snatched a tissue and wiped away the blood.

Should I feel pity? Guilt? A pinch of anger? I had no idea. All I knew was that I would keep wiping. Until I erased all of Sumire's wounds.

TABLE FOR YOU

When I told the izakaya waitress—Mutsumi, according to her name tag—that I hadn't ordered potato salad, she just left the bowl on the counter in front of me and scuttled to the kitchen. I scowled at her back. Should I call her over? No, if she didn't get my message the first time, why would she get it the second?

I was about to hail the chef, but then I peeked down at the creamy mashed potatoes, the almost luminescent carrots, the translucent slices of cucumber. A lot of effort had been put into this dish. Why not eat it?

I picked up my chopsticks and took a mouthful. The potato was softer than foam. A softness that boosted the solidity of the ham and cucumber. A softness in which salt, sugar, and vinegar, instead of being rivals, enhanced each other's flavor, or rather, gave birth to a new one.

This was the perfect potato salad.

The next day after work, I visited the izakaya again. Like yesterday, I scanned the wooden boards hanging above me, paralyzed by all the food choices. *Tamagoyaki?* No, I'd already eaten eggs for breakfast. Grilled saury? Too many fish bones. Chilled tofu? Not today; I was craving strong-flavored food.

I was still fighting my indecision when someone's head entered my field of vision. Orange yukata, loose bun, milk-white skin. It was Mutsumi, who'd placed a plate holding four pieces of prawn tempura on the counter.

"I didn't order this," I told her. "In fact, I haven't ordered yet."

She averted her chocolate eyes, nibbled at her cherry lips, then joined the chef in the kitchen without a word.

Maybe she couldn't hear or speak? No, why would someone hire a deaf waitress? Maybe she had a terrible memory? Whatever. I was craving fried food anyway.

I grabbed a prawn with my chopsticks and inspected it. The body was evenly dressed in fried flour, and it'd been straightened flawlessly, as though it'd been pulled from both ends by strings.

My mouth watering, I dipped the prawn in the tempura sauce and took a bite. The batter was so crunchy it masked the chatter of the customers while I chewed, for a moment, giving me the illusion that I was the only soul in the room. The prawn under this layer was a sponge coated with the saltiness of the sea. No strong odor. No slippery oil.

This was the perfect prawn tempura

That weekend, Mutsumi brought me a rectangular plate holding six pieces of tuna belly.

"Look," I began, locking my eyes with hers, "I don't mind eating random stuff. Heck, I'm even starting to enjoy it. Each dish is a surprise—but could you tell me why you're doing this?"

Mutsumi bit her lower lip, her eyes glued to the counter. Finally, she scurried to the kitchen like a frightened kitten.

Unsure of what to do, I inspected the tuna belly before me. It'd been cut into well-formed bite-sized rectangles. The fat made the surface sparkle, giving them the appearance of rubies.

I picked up one piece with my chopsticks and took a bite. Actually, I didn't have to chew; as soon as the sashimi made contact with my tongue, it melted like butter. And the taste was so fresh, the image of the sea—waves, whales, seaweed—flowed into my mind, simultaneously filling my heart with a new-found love for cuisine.

This was the perfect tuna belly sashimi.

Mutsumi continued serving me arbitrary dishes. Strange as it sounds, I became used to the service she provided me; or rather, I became relieved, since I no longer had to engage in staring contests with the menu.

So, I stopped asking her questions. I'd just eat, pay, and leave.

On Monday, I had octopus with wasabi—the wasabi shot ecstatically up my nose. Tuesday: grilled salmon—it didn't let down my expectations. Wednesday: calamari rings—fried just right. Thursday: pork tonkatsu—it left me drooling even after eating it.

On Friday, common sense seeped into my brain. *This is wrong. A waitress shouldn't be ordering for you, even if the food is fabulous.*

That's why, that same day, I resolved to confront Mutsumi, without leaving the place until receiving a clear response.

However, when I stepped into the izakaya, I couldn't find her. Had she taken a sick day? Cut down her shifts?

The chef attended me instead. "What would you like to order?"

"I would like to ask a question," I said. "Where's the waitress?"

The chef smoothed his vanilla-colored yukata. "Mutsumi? Unfortunately, she's not working here anymore."

"She quit?" I blurted.

His furrowed brows seemed to say, *I shouldn't divulge the details, but twisting the truth might be worse.* "I had to fire her because I saw her giving wrong orders to customers. Not only that. She was cooking the dishes herself, using my store supplies without permission. If the food couldn't be prepared discreetly, she'd lie about having received the order."

It took me a moment to process his words, and to utter mine. "She didn't tell you why she did it?"

The chef shook his head. "That's another reason I fired her."

My mind ran through his revelation again. "Wait, you said *customers*. That means she was doing this to many people?" *Not only me?* I thought with a sour heart.

"Sorry, *customer.* Singular." He squinted his small eyes until they almost disappeared. "Hey, Mutsumi was serving the food to you, right?" When I nodded, with a bow, he added, "I apologize profoundly. Mutsumi also wants to apologize."

I sprung from my chair. "In person?"

"Not exactly." The chef fished a folded note out of his yukata and handed it to me. "She wrote this letter of apology and told me to give it to you."

My eyes bounced between him and the piece of paper.

This was the perfect mystery.

I read Mutsumi's letter as soon as I stepped out of the izakaya.

Dear Tabei (sorry for making up a name for you),

Actually, this isn't an apology. It's more like a confession.

First thing I want to tell you: I can speak. I'm just not good at it. The words I choose are either too bitter or too sweet or too something. So, in the end, I swallow them down.

Writing is easier for me since I can handpick the words one by one. That said, I express myself best through cooking. Food isn't just something you eat, you know? It's also a medium of communication. Instead of words, though, you use your hands and knife, ingredients and condiments to express yourself.

That's why I cooked for you each time you came to the izakaya. I wanted to convey my feelings for you through my food. Yes, you read well. My feelings for you.

I know what you're thinking: how can I have affection for a stranger? And you're right—except you aren't a stranger to me. Excluding your name, I know a lot about you.

How you split disposable chopsticks perfectly.

How you avoid slurping your noodles.

How you tear napkins in two and use them separately (you do this to save trees, right?).

How you gaze out of the window as if waiting for your date.

How it takes you forever to choose from the menu and end up ordering the same dishes.

But you know what I like the most? How you eat. You do it with your eyes shut, as if you don't want your other senses to interfere with that of taste. As if you're making a silent prayer. As if eating is the ultimate pleasure—you know, maybe it is. Same as cooking for your sweetheart.

I hope you enjoyed my food, that it wasn't too bitter, too sweet, or too something.

Mutsumi.

"No, your food was never too bitter or too sweet," I said, salty tears traveling down my cheeks and neck. "And by the way, my name *is* Tabei."

"For the fourth time," the chef said, his back to me as he cooked in the kitchen, "I can't give you Mutsumi's address or phone. It's against policy."

"But this is an emergency," I pleaded, spreading my hands flat on the counter.

"And what that emergency might be?"

A broken heart, I almost said, but rapidly realized the stupidity of the statement.

"Look," the chef began, turning around, "maybe Mutsumi will show up here one of these days. Sure, I fired her, but we didn't end on bad terms. Plus, she loves eating izakaya food, not only cooking it."

I nodded to the chef, recalling what Mutsumi wrote in her letter. *Food is also a medium of communication.* What was she trying to tell me with her dishes? Probably the same over and over: I have feelings for you.

Putting my hopes in the chef's theory, I went to the izakaya from eight to eleven p.m. every day. For a whole week.

Mutsumi didn't show up on Monday (after almost an hour, I ordered octopus wasabi).

Nor on Tuesday (I chose grilled salmon this time).

Or Wednesday (calamari rings).

Or Thursday (pork tonkatsu).

On Friday, I stood up and said goodbye to the chef without ordering anything.

With a faded glimmer of hope, I looked around the neighborhood for Mutsumi. Since she'd worked at the izakaya every day, there was a remote chance she lived nearby. I checked parks, parking lots, pachinko parlors, all kinds of public spaces. I did this for a whole week.

On the last day of my vain search, hungry and dispirited, I switched my target to an izakaya. Why not visit the one I frequented? Because the food there would give me the same message again and again: *Mutsumi is gone for good.*

I didn't have to explore for too long. Two blocks from the old izakaya, someone had opened a new one. Framed bamboo door, fish paper lamps, a sign with Friday's special cocktails—it seemed to be a nice place.

Inside, I greeted the chef, sat on a chair at the counter, and scanned the menu. *Kaarage?* No, I'd been eating too much fried food lately. Wagyu beef?

Too expensive. Potato salad? Bad idea: it'd remind me of Mutsumi, and it surely wouldn't taste as good as hers.

I was trapped in this tornado of hesitation for almost ten minutes. When another five had passed, a pair of delicate hands put a plate of sizzling yakitori skewers before me. They were sleekly stacked, and of a carefully selected variety: chicken heart, beef tongue, shiitake mushrooms, deep fried tofu. They had the lushness of aroused lips, and the tan of someone who'd sunbathed naked at the beach the whole summer.

I looked up from my plate, smiling foolishly.

WEARING THE SKIN OF A WOMAN

Manami had never been so distressed—not only because this was her first date with a man, but also because it was the first time she would act like a woman.

Or been so stressed. The dresses Manami tried on at the clothes shop were either too tight or old-fashioned or costly. The wigs she checked out at the department store were too thick or bright-colored or itchy.

In the end, Manami borrowed a one-shoulder dress and double-strap heels from her elder sister who—aware of the occasion's weight—helped her to wear lipstick, eyeliner, fake eyelashes, and breast enhancement pads. As the cherry on top, she fitted on Manami the Sailor Venus wig she used for cosplay (her sister was a devout otaku).

"Wow," her sister chirped, eyes fixed on the Manami in the mirror. "You look like a *real* woman."

I hope Ichikawa thinks the same, Manami thought as she stood at the south entrance of Shinjuku Station, watching people stream past her on the ocean-blue pavement. At one point, she spotted a schoolgirl holding a satchel with both hands. Quickly, Manami removed her handbag from over her shoulder and replicated the girl's posture. This looked better. Cuter.

"Excuse me, are you Manami?"

She turned to face Ichikawa, who was one head taller than her, twice as muscular, and with a voice four times lower than hers. Those features—together with his small eyes, slim lips, and square jaw—made him the epitome of masculinity. His physique—along with his dark blazer, dress shirt, and denim jeans—added to the effect.

"Yes, it's me." No, that sounded too low. Manami should speak in a voice high enough to be heard from Mount Fuji.

"Sorry if I'm being rude," Ichikawa said. "But you look a bit different from your photos."

Manami's back became an iceberg. "Y-you think so?" This was the end. The Apocalypse.

"You look—how to put it?—more *feminine*."

With a short sigh, she said, "I'm glad. Thing is, I haven't updated my social media photos in years." She stroked her blonde wig. Thank god Ichikawa hadn't said she resembled an anime or manga character.

"I feel like I haven't *eaten* in years." Ichikawa pointed to the overpopulated area of the street. "Shall we go?"

Manami nodded and stepped toward Ichikawa. Wait, on what side of a man should a woman walk? On his left, in case he wanted to defend her with his strong arm, or on his right so he could protect her from traffic on left sidewalks? She couldn't decide so, despite his protests, she trailed behind him.

At the restaurant alley they'd agreed to go to, Manami spotted many izakaya with mouth-watering skewers and world-class beer. Should she pick a place? No, taking the initiative on the first date wasn't very ladylike. Also, men liked to take the lead, act chivalrous.

In the end, Ichikawa took Manami to a mini-izakaya (so they could sit closer?), the type with a bar for five to seven people. A salaryman and three women sat on the inner side, so they settled themselves on the outer. The smoldering grill, together with the pressure of making a lasting impression on her first date, made Manami perspire even from inside her ears. *Stop sweating, stop sweating. Women don't sweat like this.*

"What's wrong?" Ichikawa asked. "You didn't want to come to an izakaya?"

"That's not it," Manami replied, waving her hands in front of her.

Actually, she'd welcomed the idea of eating skewered meat since it wouldn't require her non-existent table etiquette. Holding the menu, though, she spotted another problem: how many skewers should she order? If only she could order chicken skin, pork cheek, beef tongue—everything on the menu. But her gluttony would surely leave a bad taste in Ichikawa's mouth. Therefore, she let him order the two five-skewer sets he proposed they share, as well as beer.

The latter, thankfully, loosened her body, especially her tongue. *We've been chatting for a hella long time, and I dunno what you study. Nuts, huh?* No, that wasn't the right script.

"Oh, right," Manami said in a high-pitched voice that pierced her own eardrums, "you haven't told me what your major is."

"Yeah, that's nuts. Guess we were too busy talking about living and forgot about life. Anyway, I study law."

"Oh, really?" Manami had as much interest in law as the political situation on Pluto, but a woman had to show interest in a man's career. Make him feel strong and smart, supported and successful. "What's so interesting about law?" And she sucked in that department.

"It amazes me how a few words, a few lines, can guide the behavior of a whole nation. Of the whole world. And who knows, maybe in a distant future, of the whole universe." He faced her with a guilty look. "But I don't want to be a bore. Let's talk about something else. What do you study?"

Manami drummed her artificial nails on the burnished bar. Should she tell him she studied computer science? That she participated in hackathons instead of marathons? That she used Linux instead of Windows? That she fancied Mark Zuckerberg instead of Jesse Eisenberg? Perhaps not. But what should she do then? Lie? If she planned to go a step further with Ichikawa, that might backfire.

"I study ..." she started, chasing skittish words in her head. "Digital Research and Development."

Ichikawa's monolid eyes doubled in size. "Never heard of that major."

"Only a minority of universities offer it." Manami washed her lying mouth by chugging beer, then swallowed the burp that'd gathered in her throat. "This topic isn't very interesting. Tell me more about you. What are your hobbies?"

"Let's see." Ichikawa twined his toned arms around each other. "Singing, skydiving, and sightseeing. How about you?"

"Soccer, skateboarding—I mean, shopping, sewing, and stationery."

Their beers ran dry, as did their conversation. Fortunately, the skewers— beef tongue, chicken skin, duck breast, pork liver, salmon belly—arrived. Manami grabbed a stick but dropped it immediately. Should Ichikawa go first? And after he did and she got her skewer, should she tear off the meat with her teeth? No, come on, a lady wouldn't do that. But if she used her fingers, they'd become greasy. She could use the pointy end of a skewer, but she'd have to eat the outermost piece to do that!

"You're not going to eat?" Ichikawa asked, blinking at her a couple of times.

Manami let out a heavy sigh. "I ... just remembered I'm on a diet. It's okay. I'll just drink beer."

Ichikawa chuckled. "Women care a lot about their appearance—right, speaking of that." He squinted until his eyes became two minus signs. "There's something funny here."

Manami clutched her head. Had he discovered she was wearing a wig? Oh no. His eyes lowered. Perhaps he'd found out her breasts were fake? He must've also noticed how they quivered due to her racing heart. How to stop the beatings? Preferably forever?

Ichikawa snapped his fingers soundlessly. "I know. This dress isn't yours."

Her jaw dropped ajar. "H-how do you know?"

"I grew up with two sisters. The elder used to dress the younger in her dresses. She looked beautiful in them. But they were too big. In fact, the straps kept slipping down her shoulders."

Manami pulled up her straps. "You're very observant. You'll make a good lawyer."

Ichikawa fiddled with his foggy glass of beer. "Look, don't misinterpret me, but would you like to come to my apartment? I want to show you something. Or I should say, I want *you* to show me."

"A-and w-what is that?" Was the answer obvious? Hopefully not.

"Don't worry. It's something you'll show me dressed."

Dammit. Why hadn't Manami watched the romance anime Lovely Complex with her sister instead of the friendly match between Nigeria and Argentina? Soccer didn't teach you if a man wanted to love you or just score with you.

Ichikawa slapped the back of his head, as if punishing himself. "I understand why you're having second thoughts. This is our first date after all. Please, forget I brought it up."

Manami tilted her head to the side. Maybe he wasn't a bad guy? Maybe it wouldn't be wrong to go to his apartment? She didn't have a good record of right choices.

Maybe she should let luck decide for her?

Manami had never been so embarrassed—not only because this was her first date with a man, but also because it was her first time going to his apartment.

Ichikawa lived in a run-of-the-mill, two-story building like her own. On the first floor. Good. She didn't consider herself fit enough to go up a staircase in her drunken state.

He swung the door open and turned to face Manami. "Ladies first."

Manami took off her double-strap heels—thank god, because her feet were starting to look like fists—and tiptoed into Ichikawa's apartment, which turned out to be a one-bedroom one. With the usual furnishings: table, futon, refrigerator.

The only atypical item was a closet the size of an elevator.

"Open it." Ichikawa joined her side. "Don't be polite."

Manami gave him a half nod. What was his plan? Killing her and hiding her in this closet?

There was only one way to find out.

With a trembling hand, she clasped the cold, metallic handle and pulled. Manami's eyes expanded. Inside hung an army of dresses lined in neat rows. Exhibiting various shapes: tent, trunk, triangle—dresses for all kinds of Cinderellas and Tinker Bells.

"Remember when I told you about my sisters a while ago?" Ichikawa said, probably noticing the perplexity in Manami's eyes. "It was a half-lie. My elder sister didn't dress a younger sister—because we don't have one—but *me*."

Manami's heart shrank while her mind went blank. "So you're, you're—"

"No, I'm not a crossdresser or homosexual. What happened was, my sister dreamed of having a little sister. You know, to style her hair and dress her up in clothes. So she was a bit disappointed when I was born."

He caressed a dress as though it were the ghost of a lover.

"But my sister didn't treat me badly. In fact, she was always caring and loving. That's why I tried to make her happy by being that little sister who was never born. Who gave me her ticket so I could take her place in this world."

Manami nodded. Beaming. Because Ichiwaka had opened the closet of his heart. "So, do you still wear these dresses?"

"With this hulk of a body?" he blurted. "I just keep them as souvenirs, memories from my childhood. Or I should say *girlhood*."

She asserted her head again. "They're gorgeous. It's enough to look at them."

"Trust me, it's far better to wear them." Ichikawa gestured ceremoniously to the closet. "Go on, pick any you like."

"A-are you sure?" Manami stuttered.

"I am. This is the reason I brought you here."

She nodded a third time, convinced to choose a dress. A difficult task since they were all equally beautiful. In the end, she selected the simplest one: a white A-shaped dress with no lacing or beading whatsoever. It reminded Manami of a blank sheet of paper.

After laying the dress on the low table, she slipped the straps of her own off her shoulders. Next—should she pull her dress over her head or push it past her hips? She chose the first option so her dress wouldn't mop the floor. But she must've done it too roughly, because one of her bust enhancement pad popped out and rolled onto the floor. Manami stared at herself in the closet's mirror. She looked like an unfinished sculpture. That wasn't all she saw.

She also spotted Ichikawa.

How could she forget he was standing right next to her? Perhaps the alcohol she'd drunk fogged her memory. That and never having been in a man's room.

Ichikawa picked up the skin-colored pad and passed it to Manami. "Here."

She received it, her hand extended but her eyes downcast. Now Ichikawa knew that her breasts were fake. That she was fake. What to do? Best not to move or the bear of reality would devour her.

"Don't be ashamed," Ichikawa said. "I used to dress like a girl, remember? I know about these *accessories*. Also, there's nothing wrong with small breasts, or wanting them to look bigger."

Manami glanced down. Oh right. She was exposing her underwear! Fortunately, she'd secured herself with spandex shorts. Still, still, still—

"You know, I changed my mind." Ichikawa stepped toward her until his lips tickled her ear. "I don't want to see you in a dress."

Could it be ... could it be that he desired her? As a woman? Then Manami had done a good job behaving like one.

133

He leaned back. "Look, if you think it's too fast ..."

She shook her head at the speed of light. Fortunately, her wig didn't fall off. "It isn't."

"Let's do this," Ichikawa said. "I'll go ahead, but tell me if you want to stop."

Manami failed to curb her smile. "You're so considerate."

"That's because I want you. But I don't want to do anything you don't want."

In a split second, Manami's cheeks became as hot as hell. Her brain as white as Antarctica. Her throat as dry as the Sahara. Her mouth—

Ichikawa kissed her with his slim but soft lips, then used his tongue to lure hers out of its hideout. Warm, wet, wonderful. Kissing was tastier than eating ramen noodles.

While Manami resumed describing the kiss in her mind, Ichikawa pulled her to his futon and laid her on it. Now not only his mouth was linked to her, but also his chest, his belly, his legs, his hands. These last dug themselves under her bra.

"Hey ..." Manami mumbled.

"Sorry." Ichikawa pushed himself up, keeping his hands on both sides of her head. "You want me to stop?"

"Not really—but you should've already noticed. I'm completely flat."

"I told you," he said. "There's nothing wrong with small. Also, I'm not a huge fan of big breasts. I like them more like yours."

"Okay ..." Manami clamped her eyes shut, so she wouldn't have to see Ichikawa looking at her.

While she hid behind her eyelids, he slowly removed her enhancement pads and skillfully unbuckled her bra. Her breasts froze. But soon they were warmed by Ichikawa, who sucked, licked, and nibbled at them. Oh. It felt like scratching a mosquito bite—except better, so much Manami couldn't help vocalizing her pleasure.

He must've taken her moans as a green light because, slowly, smoothly, his hand traveled down to her stomach, her abdomen, her groin–until they reached their final destination: her spandex shorts.

"Wait," Manami yelped, clutching Ichikawa's heated hand.

"Sorry," he said, still seizing her shorts. "I keep making you uncomfortable. You want me to stop?"

"T-t-the thing is ... t-today isn't a *good day*. If y-y-ou know what I mean."

Ichikawa guffawed. "You're just nervous. I can tell from your voice."

"I am ... but ..."

"But don't worry, I'll be extremely gentle." He slithered his fingers until they found the waistband of her panties.

No.

"Stop, stop!" Manami wriggled and thrashed and screamed. When she opened her eyes, she saw two colors. White: her clenched fist. And red: Ichikawa's injured nose, which she had turned into a gory faucet.

"Crap." Manami put on her dress and high heels—without bothering with her bra—snatched her handbag, and darted out of the door. She ran and ran, her tears, like a wrong pair of glasses, preventing her from seeing ahead.

But her feet must've memorized the way back because, in no time, the screech of passing trains, and the shoes of hurrying pedestrians filled her ears. Shinjuku Station. Manami bought a ticket, boarded the train, and disembarked in the station neighboring her apartment.

As soon as she reached there, she shook off her shoes and dove into the bathroom. In front of the mirror, she unpeeled the Sailor Venus wig from her head and the pins from her wiry, short hair. Finally, she shoved the wig into the drawer of her wardrobe, reminding herself to change her approach to dating—namely, staying away from it.

Oh right, Manami had to change something else. She pulled down her panties and peered down.

Her period had come like a tsunami this time. Thank god she'd stopped Ichikawa.

No, that wasn't the only reason she did it. She'd had enough of acting like a woman. Besides, faking every word, every move, seemed a real waste of energy.

After changing into a T-shirt and a pair of shorts, Manami sprawled onto her two-seater with the six-pack she'd stocked in her mini-fridge. She clicked on the TV to watch the X-Games on ESPN. However, her eyes kept flitting to her phone, which lay limply next to her.

Should she check it? Not recommendable. But her curiosity forced her to do so.

1 message from Sister.

How's the date going? You know, come to think of it, you don't need to act like a woman, because you've always been and always will be one.

With a heavy sigh, Manami texted back, *Thanks for cheering me up.* Then she scrolled down the screen.

11 messages from Ichikawa.

Should she reply to them? Probably not. But her budding affection for Ichikawa told her to do so.

Manami tapped open the first message, making a promise to herself: this time she wouldn't act like a woman. She would *be* a real one.

MY (ALMOST) LIFE AS A HIKIKOMORI

According to Japan's Ministry of Health and Welfare, I could be considered a hikikomori, since I ...

... haven't left my one-bedroom apartment in Shibuya (except to buy food and goods at FamilyMart).

... haven't joined social situations of any kind (not a hard task, since becoming a recluse drove all my friends and family away).

... haven't returned to the academic or corporate world (in other words, my studies at Keio University and my part-time job at KFC).

... don't suffer from any disease or disability (if you don't count chronic masturbation as a condition).

... and I've been living like this for at least a year.

Then what do I do during the day and night? Lately I ...

... get rid of my morning wood before one p.m. (sometimes this drags on until two p.m.).

... play video games from two p.m. to five p.m. (at my three-monitor gaming setup).

... have dinner at seven p.m. (this is my only normal activity of the day).

... get rid of my night wood before ten p.m. (often the procedure extends until eleven p.m.).

... watch anime or read manga from eleven p.m. until I pass out on my desk (I put my futon right before my chair so I can fall right on top of it).

I'm slowly leaving this pitiful lifestyle behind, though. Thanks to a drop-dead gorgeous woman called Takahashi.

I met her—or rather, she came to annoy me—one afternoon while I was playing Life is Strange in my gaming setup. The main character had just gone back in time to stop a suicide attempt when I heard a chime. It took me a few minutes to identify it as my doorbell. Not only because my speakers played at full blast, but because no one had rung it in months.

Groaning—you should never bother a man when he's playing video games—I staggered through the empty lunch boxes, beer cans, and cups of instant noodles littering the floor. Who could it be? My landlady? No, I paid my rent last week. Her husband? Improbable. I had that fling with his wife years ago. If he hadn't found out then, it was improbable he'd found out now. That only meant ...

"Are you promoting something?" I called, leaving the door closed.

"I am," replied a woman's voice, muffled by the wooden wall between us. "My product isn't tangible, though."

"If you're here to preach some religion ..."

"I don't serve gods. I serve people."

I scratched my tangled hair. If not a creed or goods, what could this woman be selling? A delivery of unsolicited sex?

Luckily, she prevented this conversation from turning into a guessing game. "My name is Takahashi. I work for the Social Reintegration Program for Hikikomori."

"What the hell is that?" I blurted.

"The Ministry of Health and Welfare is worried about the rising number of hikikomori, because they're affecting Japan's economy. So, it created a program to locate them, give them therapy, and finally bring them back to society."

"Wait, the Ministry of Health and Welfare knows what I'm doing? Or to put it better, what I'm not doing?"

"It doesn't, but I do," Takahashi said. "Each social worker in this program has their own modus operandi. In my case, I talk with apartment building owners and ask them if they have a tenant who might be a hikikomori."

"That's a breach of privacy ..."

"For the public good."

"But they give you that information?"

"Yes, after the owners learn I come from the government," she explained. "Anyhow, they welcome my job. A functioning citizen is more likely to pay the rent and stay away from trouble."

"I have no idea what you're planning to do." I directed my back to the door. "But no thank you, I don't need your services."

"Of course you do," Takahashi said. "That's why our program was created."

I faced the door one more time. "Just because something was created, it doesn't mean it's useful. For example, those mindless talk shows."

"At least talk to me a couple of minutes. Please?"

"Give up. You're not gonna talk me into it."

"Okay," Takahashi said with a subtle sigh. "If you're not going to listen to me, at least read what I have to say."

Two minutes later, I heard a sliding sound under the door. I looked down. Below me lay a pale sheet of paper. I picked it up, half curious, half cautious.

We don't have to dive into the program right away. Let's get to know each other first. I'll start.

My full name is Aika Takahashi. I'm twenty-four. I used to be a call girl in an escort agency in Kabukicho. I don't want to share too many details for obvious reasons. In short, I worked there for a long period of time. Until I almost lost my life while sleeping with a violent client.

That was my wake up call. With the help of a police officer, I got away from the agency. The same person introduced me to this job in the Ministry of Health and Welfare. The idea appealed to me immediately. Because instead of pleasing people indoors, I'd bring them outside and help them live satisfactory lives. Just like my friend did for me.

That's a brief introduction of me. Now it's your turn to share. I can't wait to hear your thoughts and feelings.

Note: write on the back of this letter and leave it under the door. I'll come back tomorrow at the same time.

Did these words come from Takahashi's heart or from a guidebook made by the Ministry of Health and Welfare? Probably the latter, since it'd been written beforehand and over-the-top.

I flipped the piece of paper over and scribbled my honest thoughts.

"You've had an interesting life, now can you leave mine alone?" Takahashi read aloud the next day, from the other side of the door. Chuckling, she commented, "We're making progress." She gave out a cough. "Unfortunately, this pace is too slow for me."

"Then maybe you can make a quick retreat?" I suggested.

After a few seconds of hollow silence, she said, "I have a better idea: I'll make a forcible entry."

Forcible entry? What was she going to do? Kick down the door? Not even a man was strong enough to do that. Shove herself through the glass door of my veranda? It was closed and only accessible from my neighbors' verandas.

One, two ... ten minutes passed. No movement. No sound.

When another minute passed, the doorbell chimed. What? This was her plan?

"You better try something smarter," I mocked, my lips brushing the door.

"Excuse me," said a low male voice. "This is food delivery."

"What?" I blurted. "I didn't order anything."

"Let me see." The man made fumbling noises, followed by whispers and pauses and repetitions. At last, he spoke again. "Let me confirm. Is this address 150-8010 Shibuya 1-18-21, Shibuya-ku, Tokyo?"

"That's ... correct." What in the name of Buddha was going on?

"Then please receive your delivery," the man said with a professional voice.

With a long sigh, I opened the door. Before me stood a hefty guy with a navy blue hat and a ruby red polo, cradling a cardboard box stamped with the letters KFC. He passed it to me and I signed the delivery recipe.

"Thank you, sir," the man said. With a slow bow, he waved his hand and ambled away—revealing a woman who'd been hiding behind him.

She was a thirty-something with porcelain-white skin, a wasp-thin waist, disk-shaped eyes, and shoulder-length hair. Damn. The Ministry of Health and Welfare was surely desperate to get hikikomori out of their apartments. Especially the pervert ones.

"Thanks for opening the door." Takahashi, who probably called delivery using my address hung outside, removed her heels and barged into my apartment.

I would have stopped her, but the litter on the floor did it first.

She poked at a lunch box with her foot, as though checking if it was still alive. "I've seen recycling centers cleaner than this."

"Thing is, I don't throw the garbage," I said, half proud, half ashamed, "because the drop-off point's too far from here."

"Don't worry, I'll help you clean." Takahashi took off her one-button coat, unveiling a double-layer blouse, and draped it carefully on my desk chair. After inspecting my apartment with a squint, she began collecting the flotsam on the floor. Every time she bent over, she exposed her pear-shaped buttocks, lovingly outlined by her small-size jeans.

"Are you sure about this?" I asked, my eyes still distracted by the seductive show in front of me.

Takahashi shot me a nod. "'Sure' as in this place 'sure' stinks.'"

True, I detested the idea of having someone in my apartment. But would it be so bad to receive free housekeeping services from a head-turning woman? Especially now that my apartment had become ridiculously filthy; I had to wash my soap every time I needed to use it, and I couldn't walk without playing soccer with a beer can.

There was only one problem: Takahashi's bombardment of questions.

"How do you cover your living expenses?" she asked, yanking down my dusty curtains. "With your savings?"

I slumped onto my futon. "With my allowance. And the tuition my parents send me—they think I'm still going to university." I hated sharing personal information with people. Not because I didn't like to share it, but because I didn't like people. But Takahashi was providing me charity, so I should donate some friendliness.

"Why did you decide to stop going?" She carried the curtains into the bathroom.

I dropped back on my futon. Had this turned into a visit to the psychologist? "I was studying biology. I chose that field because I thought it would teach me about life on Earth, or at least how it works. It didn't. So after sticking to it for a year, I decided to drop out of university."

She came back to the room. "Why didn't you change departments?"

"My major wasn't the only problem. I was sick of listening to people lecture for hours. Sick of not sleeping enough. Sick of having to go to class even when I was ill. And what for? To get a job and be even busier? More tired?"

"What about your parents?" she asked. "Aren't you worried about disappointing them?"

"I'm not usually in the mood to consider other people's feelings."

Takahashi lifted a pile of shirts from the floor. "Not even those belonging to your friends? Or I should say, past friends?"

"I've never had any," I said. "Friendship is overrated. It's just a romanticized version of 'you scratch my back and I'll scratch yours.'"

"Still, you must feel lonely sometimes ..."

"I'm not usually in the mood to consider my own feelings either."

"Maybe you should?" Takahashi suggested, tucking my dirty clothes into the washing machine on the veranda.

"You're a very talkative maid," I said.

"But a very efficient one." She continued mopping, scraping, and tidying up my apartment. After another hour of relentless cleaning, she stepped in front of me and extended her arms like a real estate agent showcasing a house. "See?"

I glanced around. Unbelievable. The walls were free of full-grown mold. The desk of half-eaten instant noodle cups. The floor of empty lunch boxes— only their cardboard counterparts. My apartment looked like when I first moved in two years ago.

"Thank you for cleaning my apartment. You did a good job." I gave her a low bow. "Now could you please leave?"

"Sure." Takahashi slid on her one-button coat and double-strap heels. Outside, returning my bow, she said, "It was a pleasure to serve you."

I said goodbye and slammed the door shut. At last, some time alone—wait a minute, her job was to help people re-enter society. Why did she accept leaving my apartment so easily?

Whatever. I peeled off my shirt and plunged into the bathroom to match the cleanliness of my apartment.

When I reached for the soap, my hand touched a plastic dent. I scanned my surroundings, finally finding out that Takahashi had discarded it. Who the hell throws soaps into the trash can?

No choice but to buy another at FamilyMart; I ambled to the veranda and fumbled inside the pocket of my faux-fur jacket. My keys weren't there. Could it be in my button-front? Neither. My slim-fit pants? Negative.

Maybe in Takahashi's one-button coat?

The next afternoon, as if it were a normal routine, Takahashi unlocked the door with my keys and intruded into my apartment. After hanging her winter coat on my desk chair, she ambled in my direction clothed in a summer dress.

"You damn thief." I rose from my futon and pointed a finger at her. "I'll report you to the Ministry of Health and Welfare."

She flashed a sinister smile. "You can try—but who do you think they will listen to? A social outcast? Or a worker who consistently outperforms her peers?"

"So you keep your schemes secret ..."

"For the public good."

"Still, you don't have the right to steal private property." I opened and closed my extended hand. "Give me back my keys."

"Okay." She assumed the strip-search position. "If you want them, come get them."

No doubt. This social servant was also a sociopath.

"All right, what do I have to do," I began, aware I'd regret this, "to have my keys back?"

"A very simple task." Takahashi dropped her arms. "Take me to a restaurant, to thank me for having cleaned your apartment."

"You should have a not-eating-with-hikikomori policy."

"You should eat."

"I will, but not with you at a restaurant," I said. "Honestly, I hate waiting for a table for hours and talking with pieces of food in my mouth."

Takahashi gripped my hoodie's sleeve and, with a tempting, teasing tone, said, "Come on, go with me."

"I'm not stepping a single foot outside." I knelt at my low table, my arms and legs crossed. "I'm not going back to society."

"Do you hate it that much?"

"You mean that to-eat-or-to-be-eaten game dressed up in business suits and office skirts? No, I don't hate it. I just don't wanna be part of it."

Takahashi joined my side. "Listen, I'm not asking you to eat anyone. Just to eat with me."

"I understand this step-by-step program," I said. "And I choose to stay away from it."

"Let's do this." She sauntered to the entrance of my apartment. There, she held the door slightly ajar. "I'll be waiting for you downstairs. You decide if you want to come—but I won't go anywhere until you do."

I scowled. "You're insane, you know that?"

"I'm passionate about my job. And passion is crazy by nature."

Shooing her with my hand, I said, "Be crazy somewhere else."

"Remember, I will be waiting for you." Takahashi unhooked her coat and disappeared behind the door (without closing it with my keys).

Blissfully alone. Finally.

At my desk, I switched on my three screens and clicked play on the anime I'd been watching lately. Blue Spring Ride. A story about a man-hating girl who meets a good-looking guy. He's not like other boys, so she agrees to go on a date with him. But after overhearing the girl talking about her hate for men, the guy stands her up.

Should I do the same with Takahashi? A glance at my phone's clock told me ten minutes had passed. So she must still be standing outside. Waiting for me.

And she would keep doing it.

I decided to watch a less romantic option: Welcome to the N.H.K. The tale of a hikikomori like me. In one episode, the schoolgirl, who wanted to help the guy to fix his hermit habits, asked him to join the psychology lesson she'd prepared for him at a park. He stood her up.

Perhaps I should watch another anime?

My next choice was Wolf Children. In it, a university girl falls in love with a werewolf. After their relationship deepened, they decided to go out together. But the werewolf was hesitant about going—since he wasn't fully human—so he made the girl wait the whole afternoon, her head buried between her knees.

Dammit. Why was every anime about girls waiting for guys?

I checked my digital clock. More than an hour had passed since Takahashi invited me for dinner.

Could she still be outside in this biting winter? Only if she wanted to become a snow woman. Anyhow, why would a people-hater like me care?

I slid on my faux-fur jacket, headed to the door, and pushed it open. Black clouds and white drizzle greeted me. Wrapping my arms around my chest to keep warm, I trotted down the outside staircase. Once on the sidewalk, I surveyed all the cardinal directions. Nothing but bicycles, billboards, and bookstores.

No, Takahashi wouldn't have waited that long. I was worrying for nothing. I was—

"You are late!" Takahashi popped out from behind a billboard. The cold had drained the blood from her already white skin, while the drizzle had darkened her already black hair.

"And you're nuts," I scolded. "What were you doing behind that billboard?"

She gave me an ear-to-ear grin. "I wanted to give you a scare, but you surprised me first by coming."

I replied with a head-to-toe glare. "Why didn't you wait with an umbrella or under a roof? You're all soaked."

"So you would worry about my health."

I groaned. "I'm more worried about your stomach. Did you eat?"

"Yes, chocolate milk!"

I dragged her up the staircase and into my apartment. Once she settled inside, I hurried to FamilyMart to buy food—a plate of maki sushi and an instant miso soup—and gave it to her. Once she was done, I passed her some of my clothes—my "Love Life" T-shirt and my only laundered shorts—and pushed her into the bathroom so she could take a warm shower. Another reason I didn't like people: you had to worry about them.

When Takahashi came out wearing my T-shirt (it looked like a poncho on her tiny frame) and my shorts (seeing them made my boxers tight), I asked, "Aren't you taking your job too seriously?"

"I told you, I'm passionate about it. Plus, I made you go out of your apartment to meet someone. I'm making progress." Takahashi let out a little sneeze.

"You're sick—physically and mentally."

"You're right. Can I lay down for a bit?" Without waiting for an official approval, she crawled until she vanished completely under my blanket.

I knelt beside her. "You're bathing in my body odor under there."

"Does it matter?" she said. "I'm already wearing your clothes."

"What if I wanna sleep?"

"Your futon is big enough." The blanket's curvy bulge slithered to one side.

Was she for real? Anyway, sleeping next to a gorgeous woman would be a dream come true.

I wriggled myself inside the blanket. As soon as I did, Takahashi hugged me from behind, locking her slender arms around my chest and pressing her squishy breasts against my back, tucking her silky legs between mine. A perfect love joint lock. She might've *actually* pleased men as a profession in the past.

"It feels nice, doesn't it?" she whispered steamily in my ear.

"Is this part of your modus operandi?" I asked.

"More like obligatory measures."

"And what's the objective?"

She increased the pressure between her chest and my back. "To make you remember how much you miss cuddling with someone."

"I don't miss it." I untangled my legs from hers. "And if I did, I'd just hug my pillow."

"It's not the same." Takahashi slipped her hand under my T-shirt and on top of my nipples. "It's not warm like this, is it?"

"Stop it," I warned, despite my boner disagreeing with me. "You're crossing the line of sexual harassment."

"Go on," she said, "report me to the police."

"This isn't a joking matter. What if *I* was the one molesting you?"

"Try it." Takahashi's plump lips curled up, tickling the lobe of my ear. "If you have the balls."

My hard-on almost poked a hole through my boxers. What was Takahashi trying to accomplish? Remind me how much I missed sex with something other than my hand? Yes, it was definitely a trap. A useless one—because I'd have jumped into the hole anyway!

After gathering enough courage, I rolled around—to face a snoring Snow White. Her relentlessness these past few days must have exhausted her. As for me, I was still full of energy. *Kinketic* Energy.

Gently but lewdly, I caressed Takahashi's uncovered thigh. Incredible. Her skin was as balmy and frictionless as the air in early summer. Would her insides be as pleasant as this? Finding out might disturb her deserved sleep.

But why would a kink-lover like me care?

With a sulky sigh, I snatched my phone, stomped to the bathroom, where I engaged in visually-aided self-gratification.

I hated it when I acted like a good person.

"You touched me last night, didn't you?" Takahashi slurped her instant noodles. Who the hell eats instant noodles for breakfast?

I slammed my cup on the low table. "You provoked me, did you forget?"

"That is the usual excuse of sex offenders," she replied in a teasing voice.

"Yeah, I am one, so you're not safe here. You should go home."

Takahashi widened her already large eyes. "I know how to make you go out!" She grabbed her napkin and began scribbling on it. When she finished, she passed it to me. I read 3 Chome-38-1 Shinjuku, Shinjuku-ku, Tokyo-to 160-0022.

"I don't know what you're planning," I said, "but I don't like it."

"You will." Takahashi stroked my leg with her socked foot. "This is the deal: if you manage to reach my apartment, you're free to turn me into your sex slave. For the whole day."

"You're joking, right?" My immediate erection told me it might not be the case.

"I used to spend my days as a call girl, remember? Besides, you already saw what I'm capable of last night." She put on her clothes—summer dress, winter coat—and opened the door. Before closing it, with her mouth lusciously agape, she said, "I'll be waiting for you at my apartment. Naked."

I seized my hard-on. No, I didn't want to make love to Takahashi. I didn't want to press her pillow-soft breasts against my chest. To glue her heart-shaped bum to my groin. To sprinkle her milk-white skin with my syrup. To—

With Takahashi's address in my hand, and after making myself presentable in front of the bathroom mirror, I put on my faux-fur jacket and pushed my way out of my apartment (without being able to lock it, but anyway, Tokyo was a relatively safe city). Downstairs, I stepped to the sidewalk and hailed a taxi. Easy.

The difficult part was about to come. At the entrance of Shibuya Station, I caught a housewife and a salaryman staring at me. They must be thinking, *What is this hikikomori doing outside? What a waste of air and sunlight.*

I bought my ticket and tucked behind the line of commuters. In front of me, a troop of girls giggled and gossiped while peeking in my direction. I could guess their conversation.

Would you date that hikikomori?

Not in a hundred years. Come to think of it, I would—because we'd both be dead by then.

This reminded me of my university days. Back then, all my classmates knew I was an otaku (the larval stage of a hikikomori), and they talked behind my back. Their words still echoed in my head.

Ichiki watches so much porn, women have to look pixelated to arouse him. Or like the 2D ones in the hentai he watches.

Speaking of 2D girls, did you know he's dating a virtual one?

Are you for real? I don't know whether to congratulate him or give him my sympathy.

As soon as the train arrived, I squeezed my way in, away from the girls and my past. This feat left me panting and perspiring, a state that worsened when I became aware of my surroundings. Heads, backs, arms, legs. People. People. People.

After a torturous eternity, the train reached Shinjuku Station. Instead of heading to Takahashi's apartment—which according to the address stood across the street—I slumped onto the bench in a nearby park to regain my energy. And most importantly, my sanity.

"I really, really, really like you," said a voice.

"Adding more really's doesn't make it more credible, you know," another commented.

On the bench beside me, I spotted a boy with a chocolate-colored hoodie and a girl with a pineapple-patterned sweater, being sickeningly sweet to each other.

Right. After I made love to Takahashi, she'd expect me to *give* her love. Once that happened, she'd invade my private space, or, god forbid, set her permanent base in my apartment. Then hell would start: walking aimlessly to national parks, eating recklessly at expensive restaurants, sitting eternally on tour buses, and traveling internationally on airplanes.

Heavens, no.

I slid Takahashi's address into my pocket and slouched my way to the subway station, still hard and glad I still had a handful of tissues in my apartment.

"How close to my apartment did you reach?" Takahashi slurped her instant noodles. If she kept visiting my home, she'd become an instant-noodle junkie like me.

"I didn't even leave mine." I lied so I wouldn't have to tell her my embarrassing episode on the streets. "I admit your proposition was tempting, but I don't lack alternative methods of erotic comfort."

"I see," she said in a contemplative tone, "not even sex will make you come out of here."

"Your eyesight's getting better."

"Okay." Leaving her cup on the table, Takahashi hurried to the futon and cocooned herself with my blanket. "If you don't leave this apartment, I won't either."

"You know that I'm stronger than you, right?" I said. "I can carry you out the apartment with my pinky."

The blanket stirred. Almost a minute later, Takahashi's marble-white arm emerged to toss out her single-stitch jeans and double-layer blouse. "If you force me outside, I'll freeze to death."

I massaged my temples. Was this person a genius or a psycho? Perhaps not the former, because I found my keys inside her jeans. Still holding them, I pondered how to chase away this pervert.

Right! Pervert.

After pulling off my chinos and putting them on the futon, I flung the blanket aside, revealing a Takahashi in a pink bra and panties. "Look, if you don't put on your clothes and leave my apartment, I'll take advantage of you. This time for real."

"Go on." She extended one pedicured toe toward me. "If you have the balls."

Driven by fury and lust, I climbed on top of Takahashi, my hands gripping her wrists while my knees immobilized her waist.

Before she could sputter anything, I parted her clamped lips with my tongue, until it entangled with hers. Oh, this steamy and slippery sensation. I'd been ages since I had the privilege to taste it. And I desired more. With one hand, I squeezed Takahashi's pillowy butt cheek. With the other, I slid her panties to the side and fondled her buttery wetness. She fed a moan into my mouth, while her tongue played with mine, my cue that I'd lost control of the game.

"This isn't working." I unlatched my lips from Takahashi's.

"What do you mean?" She vampire-sucked my neck. Then, with a come-hither look and wink, she said, "It's working really well."

I hurried to the fridge, pulled out a beer, and took a drowning gulp. How to forcibly convince Takahashi to leave my apartment? Now she crouched on the futon, still in her underwear. Seeing her, reminded me of the cold biting my skin, so I strode to the futon and put on my chinos. When I picked up my leather belt an idea struck my mind.

"Look." I slapped the belt against my palm. "If you don't leave, I'll whip you with this."

On all fours, Takahashi spun her thick rump in my direction. "I bet you don't dare."

"I'll beat you up. I don't care." I flung my belt over my shoulder, then against her. No sound of any kind.

Takahashi bent back in laughter. "You couldn't have killed a cell with that."

Rage made me strike another blow, this time drawing out a red splotch on her skin and a squeal from her mouth.

"You surrender?" I asked, guilt stinging my heart.

"I'll never back down," Takahashi said, shaking her head.

My whips resumed. By the tenth, her buttocks had become a mass of red continents. By the twentieth a red sea. By the thirtieth, her voice had become coarse. She wasn't releasing cries, though, but gasps—gasps that morphed into moans. Each longer and lower than the previous one.

I shouted in frustration.

Takahashi arched her body to glance at me. "Why did you stop?"

My belt fastened, I sulked to my gaming desk and snapped on my headset. I couldn't make Takahashi leave my apartment, but I could make her leave my mind. Or so I thought. A few seconds later, she poked my shoulder. I paused Life is Strange and spun around. She stood before me, draped in my blanket like a nun and holding a napkin that had written on it, *You don't want to play with me anymore?*

"I'm not gonna fall for your games again." I twisted back to the three screens—only to be annoyed once more by Takahashi.

Then tell me about the one you're playing in your computer, her second napkin read.

"It's about an irritating girl who has to go back to her apartment," I replied. "So she can live there happily ever after."

Does she have a prince?

"Yup, she sleeps in his futon and eats his instant noodles."

Speaking of food, could you order a delivery? I'm still hungry.

I sighed. Was starving myself the only way to get rid of Takahashi? Wait a minute.

"What a great idea!" I exclaimed, tearing off my headset.

Takahashi blinked at me. "Eating is a great idea?"

I closed the game and opened McDelivery in my browser. "I'll order a Ham and Cheese Toastie. How about you?"

She leaned toward one of the screens. "A Teriyaki Burger—with a Zero Coke and without French fries. I have to maintain my figure."

"Got it." I made the selection and clicked send.

The delivery person, a lanky guy with a red helmet and uniform, showed up in no time with our fast food. I had to close the door in his face to stop him from peeking into the apartment, probably wondering why I had a woman walking around in a blanket.

"Many thanks," Takeshi chirped from the table when I returned to the room. "I will pay you as soon as I get you out of this apartment."

I didn't join her. Instead, I dug out my toastie from its paper bag and devoured in four bites. Same with my French fries.

"I see why you liked my idea," she said. "You're starving."

"That's not the only reason." I fished out Takahashi's burger and gobbled it up. Choking, I grabbed Takahashi's Zero Coke and emptied it in one gulp.

"Those were mine ..." she uttered, staring at me as though she'd seen a coin vanishing trick. With a finger on her chin, she said, "I know what you are planning. You want to starve me to death."

"You won't die if you go out to get food."

"There's another solution." Takahashi checked under the table, inside my empty boxes, above my manga shelf, outside of the veranda. When she came back, she said, "No more instant noodles ..."

"That's right," I said, "there isn't a single grain of rice in this apartment."

"Fine. I'm on diet anyway." Leaving the blanket on the floor, she dove into the bathroom.

"What you doing?" I peered inside.

"I will drink tap water. It will keep me alive for a few weeks."

I gawked at her. "You're willing to die for your job?"

Takahashi wiped her moistened lips. "I don't work to live. I live to work."

She remained daring and determined.

Through twelve a.m.

And one a.m.

Not so much at two a.m.

"I had no idea hunger could hurt so much." Maintaining her fetal position, Takahashi lifted a trembling hand and drank her twentieth cup of water.

"Bet you're afraid now," I teased from my desk.

Takahashi shook her head. "You won't let me die."

"Why are you so sure?"

"You are stupid, pathetic, and antisocial—but you're a good person. I can feel it."

"Thanks for the ... compliment," I said. "But don't forget: I dislike people. So I don't care if you die."

"I don't care either. If I can't do my job, that means this world doesn't need me."

I gaped at Takahashi. This woman wasn't only a psycho; she also had psychological issues. Mainly suicidal tendencies.

But so what if she died? She wasn't fundamental to my life. All I needed were my slow-paced days, my faster-than-light Internet, my high-tech game station, my low-resolution porn, my American TV series, my Japanese dramas, my British rock albums. Also, my Asahi Super Dry beer, my water-based lubricant, my on-time food deliveries, my delayed rent payments, my online basic English course, my premium hentai collection, my instant noodles, my instant coffee, my instant messaging applications, my instant camera that I never used, my—

Takahashi fluttered her eyes open at seven in the morning. Probably woken by her pangs of hunger.

"Which do you want?" I knelt on the futon, cradling the rice balls I'd bought at FamilyMart. "Mayonnaise shrimp, minced chicken, miso bean paste?"

"Why?" she asked, rubbing an eye with one hand and cupping her belly with the other.

"It'd been a drag. You know, to tell the police what happened. *No, sir, I didn't kill her. She's from the Ministry of Health and Welfare and starved herself to death while trying to make me return to society.* I could get rid of your body. But I'd have to chop you into pieces and that would've messed up my apartment. Plus the sight of blood makes me queasy."

"Don't lie. You felt sorry for me." She gave me her back. "I don't need your compassion."

"Oh yeah? I don't need *you.*" True, Takahashi was probably irritable due to the lack of food. However, I'd lost my patience with her.

"Of course you do," she said. "Without me, you'll live a low and lonely life. Then die alone and abandoned."

"I would rather have that"—I dropped the rice balls and rose to my feet—"than having you another second in here!"

She stared at me with her huge eyes. They exhibited neither scorn nor sadness—just silent shock, as if she were witnessing the murder of a family member.

With that same facial expression, Takahashi slid on her jeans, blouse, and pumps.

"Hey," I blurted. "I thought you were in pain."

"I feel better now."

"What about the rice balls?"

"I don't have an appetite for them. I will go back home to cook." She hauled the door wide and, without even waving her hand or whispering a goodbye, shut it behind.

I stood there, my eyes open, but my brain shut down. Only when my mental capabilities returned did I absorb the implication of the situation.

Takahashi had left my apartment.

Weird. The result didn't bring me as much happiness as I'd expected.

At least I could rest now; I dropped onto the futon and hugged my blanket. Takahashi's peach perfume still clung to it, so strongly she might as well be lying next to me.

No, I wouldn't miss her. Why would I? Without her, I no longer had to listen to her angelic voice, or observe her amusing methods to reintegrate me to society, or look at her arousing underwear, or sleep with her ample breasts squeezing against my arm.

Okay, I would miss Takahashi a bit. But that didn't mean I couldn't continue living my life—because if I had managed to do it before meeting her, then I should be able to do the same from now on.

The following day, I returned to my old routine. In other words ...

... wake up at twelve p.m. and have instant noodles for breakfast (a bad habit I picked up from Takahashi).

... get rid of my morning wood before one p.m. (by envisioning Takahashi naked).

... play video games from two p.m. to five p.m. (so I wouldn't think about Takahashi).

... have instant noodles again for dinner at seven p.m. (out of nostalgia for Takahashi).

... get rid of my night wood before ten p.m. (thinking about Takahashi again).

All right, my routine wasn't quite mine anymore. Most of it included Takahashi.

Where could she be? Why hadn't she come to bother me? Perhaps she ...

... took some days off?

... took a trip to Hawaii with her friends?

... gave the escort agency in Kabukicho another shot?

... gave up on me?

No, she couldn't do that. After all, she was passionate about her job.

I Googled the Ministry of Health and Welfare's phone number and dialed it. If someone had told me I would do something like this one day, I'd have told them they were sick in the head.

"I'm Hashimoto," said a woman. "How may I help you?"

"Is Ms. Takahashi around?" I asked with stiff words, the result of not having used my voice for four days. "I would like to speak to her."

"Please wait a moment." The woman left me with those video-game-sounding call-waiting ringtones. Fortunately, she came back immediately, freeing me from the auditory torture. "Sorry, she hasn't come to work recently. Do you want to leave a message for her?"

I hung up the phone, replaying some of Takahashi's words in my mind.

I don't work to live. I live to work.

If I can't do my job, that means this world doesn't need me.

Without wasting another second, I barreled through the littered floor and, taking my black jacket and Takahashi's address, ventured into the freezing streets.

I bumped into many people on my way to the subway. Curiously, they weren't looking at me. They didn't care that I was a hikikomori. Or was it me who didn't care about them?

Because the only person I wanted to see—and be seen by—was Takahashi.

Since I knew half of the path, it only took me a few minutes to find her apartment, a non-descriptive four-story one like mine. Two steps at a time, I dashed up the staircase and stood before the door with the nameplate "Takahashi."

A door that wasn't locked.

Startled, I tiptoed into the apartment. Instantly, a stench assaulted my nostrils. It didn't take me long to locate its source: half-eaten rice balls, a hair-clogged bathroom sink, wringing-wet paper towels—and a human-shaped blanket on a three-quarter size bed.

A blanket stained with blood.

That meant Takahashi was ... Takahashi was—wait, what if she was wounded?

With my heart beating up in my throat, and tears stinging the back of my eyes, I clutched the blanket. However, I couldn't lift it, since deceased people repulsed me more than living ones. Also, looking at her wouldn't bring her back to life.

But what if she was actually alive?

Well, then she would soon yank the blanket away or at least poke her head to see who had intruded into her room. Yes, she couldn't be dead, because she was Aika Takahashi. Because she had been a member of the Social Reintegration Program for Hikikomori. Because she was the only person in the world I would love to hate. Because she was ... she was—

In the end, Takahashi didn't get out of the blanket. Her ghost did. She lifted herself from the futon, mumbled some otherworldly words to me, and wandered around the dimness of the apartment.

How I did I know she was a ghost? Her once rosy cheeks mimicked the white of bodies in the morgue, her hair fell in front of her face like the girl in the movie the Ring, her pajamas resembled the garments of zombies after having crawled up from the grave.

"Why are you lying on my bed?" Takahashi sat next to my feet, munching a crumbling rice ball. "Like a dead person?"

"You're alive!" I sprang toward her and clutched her shoulders. "But then how come you stink so much?"

Her cheeks became ripe peaches. "I didn't shower today, yesterday, and the day before."

"Why were you sleeping with your head under the covers?"

"I couldn't stand the smell of the room."

"What about the blood on the blanket?"

"I slipped on a rice ball and hit myself on the edge of the bed." Takahashi

151

raised a knee crusted with dried blood. "Who would have thought? Rice balls can kill you."

My eyes surveyed the apartment. "You don't have band-aids or at least tissue paper?"

Takahashi shook her head. "I haven't gone out to buy things. Or for anything else."

"But someone could've gotten into your apartment." I shot a glance to the door. "Why did you leave it open?"

She scratched her tangled, oily hair. "Did I?"

I slapped my forehead. "I hope you're at least paying attention to important stuff." Could be this the real Takahashi? For all I knew, she could've been an underpaid double. "Like your job. Or you gonna get fired."

"I won't," she said, glaring boldly at her phone on the desk, "because I quit."

I would have asked her why if I hadn't swallowed my tongue in shock.

She rested her head on my shoulder. With a sigh, she answered my silent question. "I realized—or rather, accepted—that when I started living to work, I stopped living my life. In fact, it was becoming miserable: I stopped eating properly, sleeping properly, even dreaming properly. It was even worse than when I was a call girl. At least back then, I could stay on bed longer."

I would have told her that life became easier with age. If only I could convince myself.

Instead, I said, "You know, it was the same with my part-time job. It's funny. I thought I was earning a living, but I was just investing in an early death."

Takahashi readjusted her head on my shoulder. "I see. You wouldn't have returned to society no matter what I did."

I glanced at the foreign door in front of me. Incredible. Only a few days ago, I was a hermit in my apartment. Now I was inside one that belonged to someone else. And not just any person.

"You're right," I teased with a lopsided smile. "There's nothing you could've done. Me neither."

"What about now?" She stared at her palms, her face stained with unhappiness and uncertainty. "What should we do?"

I looked at the mess made by this rookie hikikomori. Holding her greasy hand, I said, "How about we clean your apartment?"

WARMTH IN THE SUBWAY

Commuting on the subway train is the part of the day I look forward to the most, because I get to meet—or rather feel—The Warm Woman.

Today's trip starts badly. The middle-aged man standing in front of me keeps bumping his back on my nose. And it doesn't help that he's using so much cologne he smells like a pine tree. My stomach crawls up my throat with each sniff.

On my left, an office lady keeps brushing the swelling behind her skirt against my hand. I lift my arms parallel to each other, so I'm not mistaken as a pervert and taken to the nearest police box.

A solid, pointed object pokes my buttocks. I pray it's the corner of a briefcase or mobile phone.

"We have arrived at Shibuya Station. Please stand clear from the doors and move to the center of the train to enable passenger access."

When the doors slide open, a tide of commuters washes out, while another flows in: salarymen wearing windbreakers, schoolgirls reading manga, housewives holding shopping bags. Like Tetris pieces, they navigate around until finding and filling a suitable gap.

One of the people, a follically challenged businessman, lurches to where I am: a standing rail near one of the exits. He tries to create a space by nudging my messenger bag away—but I grip it as though it were my lifeline. With a heavy sigh and a wrinkled glare, he pulls back and finds himself being pushed to the wall.

I'm very sorry, my heart says to him, *but I'm reserving this place for someone.*

As though summoned by my thoughts, The Warm Woman shows up.

She steps onto the train, then inspects it with her narrow eyes which always remind me of a kitten that's just woken up from a nap.

Before she can turn in my direction, I tuck my bag between my knees to free the space I've guarded for her. Spotting it, she glides over and clutches

153

the standing rail, her hand so close to mine I could pretend to brush it by accident—but I don't because I would rather be a let-down to myself than upset her. And besides, our bodies are already touching. Shoulder to shoulder. Hip to hip.

Eventually, as she often does, The Warm Woman drops her head slightly toward me, in such a way that her chin-length, autumn-brown strands kiss my nose, fill it with their cherry blossom scent. Soon after that, her curled-up eyelashes flutter shut like butterflies going to sleep, and her lips part slightly, adopting the appearance of a budding rose.

I copy her actions and focus on her presence. On her shoulder, which caresses mine each time she exhales. On her hip, which supports me firmly despite its fragility. Especially on her warmth, which is the fluffy, perfumed kind that only women can exude. The type that can melt cold, lonely winters from men's hearts.

These elements wash away my murky feelings. Feelings created by the knowledge of the upcoming day: plodding into a concrete box without access to sunlight, bouncing from Excel spreadsheet to Excel spreadsheet, trotting from PowerPoint meeting to PowerPoint meeting, and commuting back to my lonely apartment in a cramped—

"We have arrived at Harajuku Station ..."

As the train slows down to stop, The Warm Woman bumps her head against my shoulder.

"I'm sorry," she utters, addressing the buttons of my shirt.

Once again, I have slim faith that she will lift her thin eyes to meet mine. That we'll look at each other for more seconds than strangers are allowed to.

"It's okay," I would tell her, blowing away the awkward silence. "It wasn't intentional."

And she'd reply, "But I'm doing it every time—or I should say, every day."

"Oh," I would blurt, feigning surprise. "I didn't even notice."

Keeping her gaze downcast, she'd tell me, "Right, why would you focus on me? It's not that I'm special or anything."

That would be my chance to say, "Actually, you're not very far off ..."

But of course, The Warm Woman just leans back and remains next to me. Her eyes, instead of aligning with mine, blink until they close, while her head levitates toward me as if by magic.

She loses her balance again in two other stations; however, she seems to have learned her lesson, because she holds tight to the standing rail, stopping herself from shoving me on the shoulder. Which is a pity.

The next station, Shin-Okubo Station, is where she gets off. And the most painful part of my trip.

Like a master in the art of train-napping, she snaps her eyes open, and turning them into two underscores, she scans the digital announcement on the wall. When the doors slide to the sides, she detaches her shoulder and hip from mine (she might as well have yanked a warm blanket from me), snatches her handbag, and apologizes her way to the line.

She stands on the third row from the door, then on the second, then on the first.

Then there's no line anymore.

Once more, I bite back the urge to shove my way out of the train. But what would I do once I caught up with The Warm Woman? Tap her on the shoulder and say, *I'm the guy who naps next to you on the train. We exchange warmth every day. How about we exchange words from now on?*

Or I could follow her to find out what she does. But I would risk coming off as a stalker, or worse, being late for work and getting kicked out of the office. If that happened, I would no longer need to ride the subway with her.

Defeated and disheartened, I lean against the standing rail and sigh. Now that The Warm Woman isn't here, I'm at this cold city's mercy. The cold of concrete buildings, metallic briefcases, ironed suits, and averted eyes. But this is the life I chose, so when my station arrives, I dive into it head-first and head-on.

As I enter the train this evening after work, I'm greeted by what could've been the whole population of Tokyo. Everyone is present. Except the only person I want here.

To comfort myself, I recall The Warm Woman in scenes clumsily filmed by my mind.

The one I remember first was recorded two days ago. The train was so packed it would've made a tin of sardines look roomy. Amidst this chaos, The Warm Woman was pushed off the railing and hard against me. I could still remember her breathing tickling my chest like a feather, her breasts acting as a cushion for my abdomen, her smell transporting me into a garden of sakura. That was my first time being so close to her.

But a sudden thought interrupted my joy: she must be asphyxiating.

"Are you okay?" I inquired.

No reply. Panicking, I summoned the superhuman strength needed to lean back, pushing the mob behind me until I could see her face. A sleeping one. With a sigh, I bowed an apology to the people behind me and continued serving as a vertical mattress for The Warm Woman. A dream come true.

I smile foolishly at my favorite memory. What I'll never forget, though, are the first days I started noticing her. And my world stopped in its tracks.

The morning I met the Warm Woman, I'd done the opposite of oversleeping: I'd woken up too early. At seven. *Anyhow,* I thought as I ambled to the subway, *better be an early bird than a fired one.*

I stepped into a jammed train, a problem that worsened after it stopped in Shibuya Station and a tsunami of people crashed in. Luckily, I'd secured a spot. Just as everyone else.

Well, except for one person: a woman—probably in her mid-twenties like me—who stood wobbly at the center of the car. Concerned, I surveyed my surroundings. The only available space was the one occupied by my messenger bag. I would indicate this to the woman, but I didn't know whether that would label me as a gent or a creep.

What if I let her know without words?

I lifted my messenger bag and banged its metallic buckle against the standing rail. *Clink.* Rapidly, I sandwiched my bag with my knees and pretended to peer out of the window, a useless move since I could already feel everyone's eyes throwing darts in my direction. Embarrassment made me shake the pole—wait, the tremor wasn't coming from me.

When I raised my gaze, on my left, I saw eyes that resembled that of a yawning cat. Skin almost as translucent as freshly laundered bed sheets. Two side flicks curling inward like twin half-moons, cradling round powdered cheeks.

It was her.

We stayed side by side. At some point during the trip, our shoulders and hips aligned together, becoming bridges for our warmth. I wasn't sure who had leaned against the other person, only that her touch was special. Like she'd shared one side of her scarf with me. Unfortunately, or rather inevitably, she disembarked the train at Shin-Okubo Station, leaving me with a glacial cold, one that I would never be able to melt.

Unless I met her again.

Bewitched by this idea, the next morning, I woke up at seven. Washed, brushed, dressed. Then rushed to the subway. Two minutes later, spirited and perspiring, I slipped onto the train and leaned at yesterday's standing rail, which to my surprise was vacant again. Probably because it was close to an exit, and therefore, at the mercy of the waves of people breaking in.

My eyes hunted for her among the human surf: students, salarymen, and other strangers. But she never surfaced. Right. I'd forgotten that I lived in a city of thirteen million people and that finding that one person twice would be like winning the lottery.

I must have bought the right tickets because, a few seconds and centimeters before the door closed, she hurried onto the train. Worshiping my luck, I watched her as she staggered to the middle of the car and peeked around. Should I hit the pole with my bag like I did last time? No, that could bring to light my intentions.

Perhaps she would check the empty spot she'd found yesterday?

My hypothesis was correct: the woman squinted in my direction and squeezed her way until she anchored by my side. I was elated. Ecstatic. However, I couldn't help but wonder why, against all the odds in the world, my wish had materialized into reality.

This question grew in size the next day, when I bumped into her on the same subway line, at the same time, and at the same standing rail—a miracle that repeated itself the day after that, and the day after that. In the end, though, delight overshadowed my doubts. After all, if I was happy, did it really matter how or why?

Two months have passed since I met The Warm Woman. Despite that, we haven't exchanged a single word other than her head-low apologies and the ones in my one-sided fantasies.

And worse of all—saddest of all—I don't know anything about her. Her name. Her surname. Her age. Her bra size. What makes her laugh. What makes her cry. What kind of things she makes with her hands. Whether she has a boyfriend. Whether she has a girlfriend. Whether she has someone with whom she can spend silent time with. If she has dreams. If she suffers from nightmares.

If she has noticed the guy she indirectly sleeps with every morning. The guy who doesn't mind serving as her pillow in the subway.

Even if I don't know the answer to any of these questions, I'll keep being that: her pillow. Because I have this microscopic hope that my dream will come true, that she will one day tell me hers. That we will share more than warmth.

"I'm sorry," mutters a strangely familiar voice.

When my eyes open, they meet The Warm Woman's, which, for the first time, are directed at me. I can see myself reflected in their blackness: a paralyzed man who doesn't know whether to feel tense, timid, or terrified—or whether these emotions have blended into one. Into a cocktail of emotions too strong for him.

In a feeble attempt to flee from fear, I switch my focus to my surroundings. I'm on one of the train's seats, sitting side by side with The Warm Woman.

Right. Today, while we were standing in our usual spot, she suddenly ambled away and sat in the far back. I panicked. *She found out about my weird pleasure,* I thought. *And now she thinks I'm a subway creep. A warmth thief.* But then I came up with a simpler explanation: she wanted to rest her feet, a rare privilege in this rush hour, only made possible, perhaps, by the recent flu outbreak.

"I'm sorry," The Warm Woman repeats, pulling me back to the present, "I don't mind having your head on my shoulder, but it was starting to get sore."

I stare at her, while my cloud of confusion slowly clears. That's right. When she sat here, I noticed that the seat next to hers was empty. Before I could lift a foot, the logical part of my brain nudged me with a question: what if she found out I was following her? But it was chased away by a fact: destiny—or the randomness of the universe—may not grant me this

157

opportunity again.

"Oh no," I blurt, "I'm the one who should apologize. I shouldn't have leaned on your shoulder." So I fell asleep? Odd. My drumming heart should've prevented that from happening.

"It's all right." The Warm Woman gives me a tilted smile. "It's not a crime to fall asleep."

"But I did it on you, without your permission ..."

"That's true." She lowers her head, her hands folding the hem of her skirt. "But it can be nice to feel the touch of a stranger, don't you think? Sometimes we don't even get that from friends or family."

"Sure," I reply, taken aback by her sudden openness. "But I'm sure you don't have that problem." People must enjoy orbiting around her. After all, she was as bright and warm as the sun.

Her narrow eyes tour their surroundings. "You're right. But weird, even though I'm surrounded by people, none of them feel close to me. I think it's because they are too many, so there's no space for them—or me—to draw near." She refocuses her attention to my face. "Has this ever happened to you?"

The Warm Woman is sharing a lot with me. Could this be a cry for help? Or a hint of contentment? Either way, I'm not going to stop this conversation here. Just the opposite. I'll catch up with her pace.

"No," I say. "At least not recently. You see, I've been living a lonely life for a while—guess I've been pushing people away."

Sensing the obvious question bubbling up in her, I continue.

"I avoid them because I worry they'll get in between me and my destination. Which is funny, because that destination—my career, my job—is not something I want to do with my life. It's just something I do to stay alive and keep doing it." I face her again, my heart pounding in my temples. "But you know, someone made me realize I miss human warmth."

She greets my eyes with curved-up lips. Their blood-red tint is a luscious contrast to her cotton-white skin. "That person must be happy. For making such an impact in your life."

"The truth is," I begin, "she has no idea about all this."

"That sounds like a sad story." The Warm Woman glances at the dark window. "And very similar to mine."

"Would you ... mind sharing it?" I ask.

"Not at all." She leans closer, which could be an illusion woven by my excitement. "We don't seem to be strangers anymore."

"Guess we are not ..." Wait, when do people go from being strangers to nonstrangers? And if there's a middle zone, what is it called? Anyhow, the journey doesn't matter anymore, only the place I have arrived.

"I also have someone," The Warm Woman starts, "someone who reminded me that I miss people's warmth, and that I'm freezing without it.

That person has become my blanket in this world. No, more than that: my bonfire."

"But he—or she—doesn't know anything about this?" Could that person be ...?

"I used to think that." She strokes her V-shaped chin and, locking her single-fold eyes with mine, she says, "But I'm not sure anymore."

My mind dissects the meaning of her words, while my heart whispers a secret to my ears. No, an undeniable fact: that The Warm Woman and I had not only been sharing body heat. It's a truth so big, I can't hide it inside.

"We are those *someones,* right?" I utter with a voice like feet testing the water.

To my enormous relief, she receives my half-question, half-statement with a smile. "I thought you'd never figure it out."

"Wait, that means you knew all along that I ..."

The Warm Woman nods. "It's quite obvious, don't you think? Every day you are at the same standing pole, at the same time, and in the same position."

"And does it bother you? You know, that we make physical contact?"

"What bothers me is not having your contact information." She wriggles herself closer to me. Definitely not a mirage created by my desires. "To go a step further. Not just commute together."

"This isn't ... too fast for you?"

"Perhaps a little," she says, doing origami with her skirt again, "but once a train departs, it can't turn around, right?"

Does this mean our story will have a happy ending? But real life doesn't have those; it keeps going on and on even after the wedding, the breakup—sometimes it gets stuck in a boring middle. And sometimes it never starts: soulmates never meet, dispassionate spouses never separate, lonely people never get to heal each other with their company.

This tale would only end happily, or just end, if all this was fictitious. Or a drea—

"We have arrived at Shinjuku Station ..."

When I open my eyes, the first images that filter in are the pale ceiling of the subway train and the dark sea of commuters. I groan. I was dreaming, being fooled by Morpheus.

And I must've been sleeping in an odd position, because my left shoulder is heavy, hurting, and—hot?

I turn to my side to see, in close-up, wood-brown hair, milk-white skin, and blood-red lips. The Warm Woman. But what happened? Oh right, I *did* sit beside her. And despite being nervous and joyous, I fell asleep. Waking up at seven was still too early for me, and I've already gotten used to napping on the train.

It's probably the same case with The Warm Woman, who is still using my shoulder as a pillow. Refusing to let this dream opportunity pass, I close my eyes and lean my head so that hers rests in the crook of my neck, caressing it and warming it at the same time.

Excitement floods my veins. And for good reason; after all, sleeping with someone—in the literal sense—is one of the most intimate activities you can do with that person.

However, I fail to fall asleep since I just woke up, and because a question is tugging me again and again back to wakefulness: what if The Warm Woman in my dream shares the same thoughts and feelings as the one sleeping next to me?

"We've arrived at Shin-Okubo Station ..." says the announcement.

In a blink of a second, she opens her eyes, and with a bowed head, she whispers, "I'm sorry." Before I can tell her that it's okay, that she could sleep on my shoulder through all the stations in Tokyo, she smooths out her skirt and slides off the seat, leaving a hollow in my neck. And my heart.

As I watch The Warm Woman in line with the other commuters, my mind tells me, *That dream wasn't a dream. It was a sign. A green light.*

She stands on the third row from the door.

You found her among the thirteen million people who live in this city. Will you be able to live with yourself if you let her go?

Then in the second row.

She's the only person you don't want to push away—because you don't see her as someone who's getting in the way between you and your destination. She is your destination.

Then in the first row.

"Warm Woman!" As soon as the words leave my mouth and she exits the train, I remember the bitter reality: that's not her name. And I have another revelation: talking to her is futile, because no matter how many times I think about her, how many times I see her, how many times I nap next to her, she will still regard me as a stranger.

And perhaps I should continue being one, because if I speak to her and spook her, I may lose my precious corner beside her. No, I couldn't take that risk; better keep my mouth and eyes shut. And keep dreaming.

The summer heat has turned my shirt and skirt into a second coat of skin. That and having to comb my hair, apply makeup, and eat breakfast faster than the subway train I'm boarding.

My body dampens even more as I wade through a river of people—past a schoolboy who likes to play mobile games, a businessman who likes to stand in front of others, and an office lady who looks like a model. This routine is almost as stressing as my job. But I bear with it because killing yourself working is a legal requirement, because the only kind of life I know is the one that goes forward.

But above all, because I get to see The Warm Fellow.

As usual, he is at the standing pole next to the doors, his large eyes inspecting their surroundings, eyes that always remind me of a puppy that's done a misdeed.

I glance around too. Not to mirror his movements, but to hide the fact that his side is the only place I want to occupy. He should've already figured out that this is an act, though, or at least thought: *I run into this woman every day. It can't be a coincidence.*

But the only way I know is the one that goes forward, so I excuse my way to The Warm Fellow until I reach his left. Right after that, I close my eyes and pretend to sleep.

When I first saw him, I thought he had saved this space for me and tried to let me know by whacking the standing pole with his bag. Instantly, I wrote off that possibility as wishful thinking and feelings. He must've accidentally hit the pole when—maybe to relieve a sore spot—he put his bag between his legs.

Still, at the time, I enjoyed his seductive shoulder, his protective build, his maple scent. But mostly, his warmth, which seemed—at least through my rosy lens—as if he had offered it. As if he'd let me have his jacket. That thought made me accept him entirely, a feat I wouldn't have repeated with another stranger. This was also the reason, together with the fact that I saw him every day, that I started to crave more than his heat.

And so, I made attempts to get closer to him.

Like one morning, when the train was more crowded than usual, I pretended to lose grip on the standing pole and be shoved to his chest. To blanket my embarrassment, I faked falling asleep. I must've done it too well because I ended up sleeping for real. Or maybe it was his soft yet solid chest, which at that moment became my safest place in the world. And the warmest one.

Unfortunately, a couple of dream seconds later, the train stopped in Shin-Okubo Station and shook me out of my cozy slumber. Apologizing to him, I darted toward the doors, cursing myself for not having taken advantage of the proximity.

Another time—actually, only yesterday—when the train was less full than usual, I spotted two empty seats, and an idea seeped into me: I would sit on one of them. Once I did, The Warm Fellow would notice its available conjoined twin and take it. It worked. And as soon as he slumped down, I prepared for the second part of my plot: pretend to fall asleep on his shoulder—but that would be a familiar commuting scene.

Hence, I decided to go the opposite way. I would wait until he began to doze off like he always did, then, with a skittish smile, tell him, "You can sleep on my shoulder if you want."

This scheme was perfect, except I fell asleep first, into a dream where we were sitting in these same seats. Talking. I don't remember what about, only that I wanted the train to skip every station in Tokyo.

That didn't happen. I caught the words "Shin-Okubo Station" and woke up. On the shoulder of The Warm Fellow. After stuttering an apology, I sprang from the seat and sprinted toward the exiting commuters. While waiting in line, I seemed to have heard someone shout, "Warm Woman," but surely it was just my imagination mocking me. Who else besides me would come up with silly nicknames like that one?

And so those—together with figuring his commuting schedule and hitting his shoulders with my head now and then—were my pathetic efforts to close the gap between The Warm Fellow and me. Maybe those failures were a sign. A red light telling me that, even though we travel in the same direction every day, we are not meant to cross each others' paths.

Yes, maybe I should remain a stranger to this man. A man I don't know anything about. His name. His nickname. His address. His blood type. What makes him proud. What makes him ashamed. What type of faces he makes when he is sleeping. Whether he has a wife. Whether he has an affair. Whether he has someone who recharges his batteries by hugging him. If he has dreams. If he takes naps in the afternoon.

If he has noticed the woman who dreams of waking up by his side one day. The woman who wouldn't mind sharing a pillow with him.

I have no idea of any of this. All I know is the warmth he gives me every day. The warmth that has become my sun in the morning, that lingers on me throughout the afternoon, that protects me from cold at night. That keeps me going in this fast-paced city.

ABOUT THE AUTHOR

Alexandro Chen was born and raised in Chile and moved to Taiwan in 2006 to study Foreign Languages and Literature. During this period, he taught English at a cram school. He's an active member on Medium, where he reads and publishes stories regularly. He currently lives in Taipei, Taiwan, where he writes novels, short stories, and everything in between. My (Almost) Life as a Hikikomori is his first short story collection.

To read more stories by Alexandro, visit: medium.com/@alexandrochen
To find out more about his editor, Diamaya Dawn, go to:
www.diamayadawn.com

Printed in Great Britain
by Amazon

32283433R00092